"Is this your idea of a bad joke?" Rick asked.

Natalie carefully studied his reaction. It was too similar to what her own reaction had been when she'd learned about her test results. She'd expected...what? An explanation that would cause all of this to make sense? However, it was obvious that Rick didn't have any answers.

"How did this happen?" he amended.

She'd already asked herself that. At least a dozen times. And she knew that Rick was not a part of this – he wasn't the sort of man that required drugging or any coercion to get a woman into bed. She didn't know how it happened and her only clue was that surveillance video.

"I don't know what happened. I need answers and that's why I am ~~h~~ ~~because~~ I am pregnant with

Available in September 2007 from Mills & Boon® Intrigue

Covert Conception

DELORES FOSSEN

MILLS & BOON

Pure reading pleasure

First published in Great Britain 2007
by Harlequin Mills & Boon Limited,
Eton House, 18-24 Paradise Road, Richmond, Surrey TW9 1SR

ISBN: 978 0 263 85747 4

46-0907

Harlequin Mills & Boon policy is to use papers that are natural, renewable and recyclable products and made from wood grown in sustainable forests. The logging and manufacturing processes conform to the legal environmental regulations of the country of origin.

Printed and bound in Spain
by Litografia Rosés S.A., Barcelona

To Rickey.
I can never thank you enough.

DELORES FOSSEN

Imagine a family tree that includes Texas cowboys, Choctaw and Cherokee Indians, a Louisiana pirate and a Scottish rebel who battled side by side with William Wallace. With ancestors like that, it's easy to understand why Texas author and former US Air Force captain Delores Fossen feels as if she was genetically predisposed to writing romances. Along the way to fulfilling her DNA destiny, Delores married an air force top gun who just happens to be of Viking descent. With all those romantic bases covered, she doesn't have to look too far for inspiration.

CAST OF CHARACTERS

Natalie Sinclair – Someone drugged her and her nemesis, Rick Gravari, so they'd have sex. Now, pregnant with Rick's child, someone wants them both dead and Rick is her only hope. Can they overcome a bitter past and work together to save their child?

Rick Gravari – He's more comfortable building custom motorcycles than he is in Natalie's high-society world. But he'll do whatever it takes to keep Natalie and his baby safe…even if that means moving in with the very woman he's sworn to resist.

Dr Claude Benjamin – Creator of the Cyrene Project, a plan to produce genetically superior babies. Can the doctor have changed his mind about continuing his research, and does he now want to eliminate them all?

Dr Isabella Henderson – She also worked on the Cyrene Project, but now vehemently objects to it.

Carlton Gravari – How far will Rick's uncle go to put an end to the Cyrene Project?

Macy Sinclair – Is Natalie's flamboyant mother covering for someone, or is she too the victim of the Cyrene Project?

Troy Jackson – A product of the Cyrene Project, he holds a grudge against Rick and Natalie.

Brandon Steven – He has answers that Rick and Natalie need, but he's not willing to share.

Chapter One

San Antonio, Texas

"You're pregnant, Natalie."

Natalie Sinclair blinked, stared at her sister, Kitt, and then waited because she was certain that Kitt was about to deliver the punch line of a silly joke.

But the punch line didn't come.

Judging from Kitt's expression, she was serious. However, Natalie was serious, too, and she knew for a fact there was no way she could be carrying a child.

"I haven't had sex in over a year," Natalie admitted. Though her sister no doubt already knew that. And it was the realization of the *no doubt* that caused any remaining amusement to vanish.

Pulling in her breath, Natalie set her teacup aside, the delicate bone china rattling against the saucer. Some of the Irish blend splashed onto a pair of entwined hand-painted yellow roses.

"Dr. Benjamin did the pregnancy test," Kitt continued, her voice shaky and thin. "He called when you were in the meeting with the antique broker, and when I pressed him about what was wrong with you, he finally told me. You don't have the flu, and you're not anemic—"

"Stop right there. I can't be pregnant." Natalie waited for Kitt to agree to that, but her sister made no such acknowledgement. In fact, nothing about Kitt's ultra-solemn expression changed. "But you think I am?"

Kitt nodded.

Okay. This obviously wasn't some joke. Besides, Kitt wasn't a joking kind of person. Still, there was no way this could be true.

No way.

Natalie shook her head. "The test is wrong."

Kitt did some head-shaking of her own. "The doctor used your blood and urine samples to repeat it. Not once. But twice. And then he repeated it again at my request. All three times, the tests were positive. Based on the physical he gave you and those test results, Dr. Benjamin thinks you're about four weeks pregnant."

Forcing herself to remain calm and think this through, Natalie snapped her fingers in rapid succession. "I've heard about this sort of thing. They're false-positive results. They have to be."

Natalie was well aware that she sounded desperate.

And she was.

What was going on here?

Kitt didn't respond to her false-positive theory. Instead, her sister turned the computer monitor around to face Natalie and typed in something on the keyboard. "You remember a couple of months ago I had surveillance cameras installed throughout the house?"

"Of course, I remember. Some items were missing, and we thought someone on the staff might be stealing from us. The surveillance tapes proved it." And Natalie wasn't pleased about this seemingly mundane topic when they had something not so mundane to clear up.

"I didn't have the cameras removed after the problem was resolved," Kitt continued. "I figured the extra security wouldn't hurt."

Impatient, Natalie huffed. "Is this leading somewhere, Kitt?"

"Unfortunately, yes. After I finished my conversation with Dr. Benjamin, I went back through the surveillance tapes for the past four weeks. I found something."

Oh.

That nearly stopped Natalie's heart.

"Explain *something*," Natalie insisted.

Kitt typed in a code on the keyboard, and Natalie instantly recognized the video feed that appeared on the screen. Nearly a month earlier.

The night of her surprise twenty-ninth birthday party.

Though Natalie was familiar with the scene, it wasn't an entirely pleasant memory. She'd arrived back in San Antonio from a week-long antique-buying trip in Ireland and had stopped by Dr. Benjamin's office because she was sick. The diagnosis was an upper respiratory infection. The doctor had done some lab tests and given her prescription meds. By the time she made it home, she had been exhausted, ready to fall face-first into bed. Only instead of bed, she'd discovered that her mother had assembled three dozen or so of her close and not-so-close friends for a surprise birthday celebration.

"Are you saying this is when the so-called pregnancy happened?" Natalie asked. "Because, trust me, I would have remembered something as monumental as having sex with one of the guests."

Though Natalie had to admit to herself that some of the night was a complete blur. She blamed the big blur on the prescription meds. Of course, the fatigue from the business trip hadn't helped, either. She'd felt like a zombie throughout the entire party. Still, her zombie-haze wouldn't explain that pregnancy test.

"Just watch," Kitt instructed.

Even with Kitt fast-forwarding the event, Natalie had no trouble spotting her mother, Macy, in the crowd that had gathered in the foyer to say their goodbyes. With her Marilyn Monroe platinum-blond hair, curvy body and dazzling smile, Macy had a way of monopolizing space and drawing attention to herself.

Then, Natalie spotted someone else.

Rick Gravari.

She automatically frowned. Rick had a way of monopolizing space as well, but in a totally different way. Wearing jeans and a white shirt, he appeared his usual self. Aloof. Surly. Her mother had no doubt invited him, but he definitely fell into the unwanted-guest category. Natalie had spent the evening avoiding and ignoring him, and was thankful he'd done the same to her.

Natalie dismissed her surly, jeans-wearing nemesis and continued to study the surveillance tape. As the guests idled by the front door, she managed to locate herself. Alone. Her head down with her chin practically touching her chest. Leaning against the wall next to the fireplace. She definitely wasn't in the throes of having wild sex.

The video stopped, and a second later, the screen became blank.

"Something went wrong with the surveillance equipment at this point," Kitt explained. "I'm not sure what. But that's not the only camera we had in operation that night." Kitt typed in something else on the keyboard. "The lighting isn't very good, but here's some footage taken from the hall outside your bedroom. The time lapse is about a half hour from the segment you were just watching."

The hall was indeed poorly lit. And empty. It didn't stay that way for long. Natalie soon saw the approaching couple. Mere shadows moving within the shadows.

"There's no camera in your bedroom so this is all we have," Kitt explained. She latched onto her Texas A&M coffee mug, took a long drink of the heavily scented espresso, and that's when Natalie noticed that her sister's hand was trembling. "Still, I think it's enough."

"Well, it's not much."

Natalie couldn't see the faces of the couple, and without audio, she couldn't tell who was approaching her bedroom door. At least, she couldn't tell until the figures got closer to the camera.

Then, Natalie realized that *she* was one of those shadowy figures.

Seeing herself, however, didn't jog any memories. She had absolutely no recollection of being in the hallway that night though she was certainly aware it'd happened. After all, she had woken up in bed the following morning.

Alone.

Still, hadn't she had a feeling that something was wrong? A feeling she'd dismissed.

Maybe she shouldn't have.

And with that uncomfortable thought repeating in her head, Natalie moved to the edge of her seat, closer to the monitor. And she studied every inch of the screen.

Praying. Hoping. That whatever image appeared, there would be a plausible explanation for it.

Natalie watched herself as she slowly approached her bedroom. The person walking beside her had his arm looped around her waist.

It was definitely a man.

He was at least a head taller than she was and outsized her by at least fifty pounds. And neither of them was too steady. When she reached the door, she staggered forward, and her arm rammed into the wall. The reaction on her face could have been either pain or giddiness.

Sweet heaven, she acted drunk.

But she knew for a fact that she'd consumed no alcohol that night. The only thing she'd had to drink was a glass of sparkling fruit juice that someone on the catering staff had gotten for her shortly after she arrived home.

"Okay, here it is," Kitt said.

Natalie waited and watched. The man in the video turned, shifting his weight. So did Natalie, except she wasn't as graceful. He barely managed to catch her before she stumbled again. Once he had her semi-steady, he kissed her. She didn't resist. In fact, she kissed him back and groped behind her to open her bedroom door. And that's when the security camera and the meager lighting worked together to catch his face.

Kitt froze the image. Not that Natalie needed a second look to know who he was.

The man taking her into her bedroom was the one person on earth she considered her enemy.

Rick Gravari.

Chapter Two

Rick Gravari pushed himself away from the custom Harley he was building and glanced at the Pennzoil clock mounted on the back wall of his shop.

It was already past five-thirty.

Less than an hour to closing time, and there was at least a half day's work left to do.

"Hell," Rick grumbled.

He used his forearm to mop the sweat from his forehead and neck, and then he cursed the air-conditioning. Why had it picked the hottest day of the year to go out?

There wasn't much of a chance he'd get any of his four mechanics to stay late. Not on a Saturday. And not with the broken air conditioner. Overtime, a pizza and complete use of every fan in the place might be enough enticement for Hal, the head mechanic, but it'd be midnight before Hal and he could finish all the service orders on their own.

The phone rang, again, and Rick walked through the motorcycle clutter, fans and tools toward his equally cluttered office. Along the way, he grabbed a bottle of water from the fridge, drank some and poured the rest over his head. The cold liquid snaked down his face and back.

It didn't help.

Slinging off the excess water, he snatched up the phone from his desk and grabbed a service order so he could close out the Harley job. A little multi-tasking might get him out of here a few minutes earlier.

The caller was the soon-to-be owner of a custom bike who said he wouldn't be able to pick it up until at least Wednesday. Rick considered it a blessing. One down, too many to go.

Most days, he loved his job. He loved having his own business. Loved working with his hands to build custom motorcycles and repair them.

But today wasn't one of those days.

"Hey, Rick? You'll wanta take a look at this," Hal called out when Rick hung up the phone.

Hoping they weren't about to get another customer, whom he'd almost certainly have to turn away, Rick glanced through the porthole-shaped window that separated his office from the reception-waiting area. The only person there was Bennie, one of the mechanics, who was at the cash register ringing up a client.

"In the front parking lot," Hal added.

Before the last syllable had left Hal's mouth, Rick was already looking in that direction. Specifically at the vehicle that'd just pulled up in front of the shop. A sleek platinum-colored sports car. As expensive as they came.

The driver's door eased open, and thanks to the tinted window and the door itself, the only thing Rick saw of their visitor was a foot. One wearing a sexy, three-inch heel that was almost the same color as the car.

It was like watching a striptease. A delicate hand slid over the top of the driver's-side window and door. Perfectly manicured nails—the color of ripe raspberries—gripped the glass and metal. The other foot touched down on the concrete. Graceful. Like a dancer getting ready to strut her stuff.

Rick felt like fanning himself, and it wasn't all a result of the broken A/C, either. It'd been a while since he'd taken the time to appreciate the sight of a woman. This was a reminder that he truly needed a life outside the shop.

Correction: he needed a life, period.

Inch by inch, the top of their visitor's head came into view as she rose from the seat. Honey-blond hair cut short and choppy. Fashionable but not overly done. It still looked touchable, and he could almost feel his fingers sliding through it.

But then, the striptease came to a non-gratifying, abrupt halt.

Rick's gaze landed on her mouth. A full, sensual mouth covered with just enough gloss to make it noticeable. And notice it he did. Even though he hadn't immediately recognized the hair, he knew that mouth. It was the mouth of a woman he hadn't expected to show up at his shop. A woman he definitely didn't want to see. Not now. Not ever.

Natalie Sinclair.

She used her elbow to push the car door shut, eased off her sunglasses and started toward the shop entrance. No cautious footsteps for her. Just the long determined stride of a woman who appeared to be on some sort of a mission.

The muggy summer breeze flirted with her turquoise suit, fluttering the slim skirt around the tops of her knees. And even slightly higher. He saw a good portion of her toned and tanned right thigh. Rick obviously wasn't the only one to notice that because Hal mumbled something about being in lust.

Rick understood completely.

He felt the lust.

And he wanted to kick himself hard for feeling it.

Thank goodness that lust was tempered with a hefty dose of reality and vivid, godawful memories. That lust had already cost a man his life, and it didn't matter how good she looked, Rick had made a solemn promise that he'd have no part of Natalie Sinclair.

Now, the question was—did she want a part of him?

He didn't mean that in a sexual sense, either. Rick

knew Natalie would never think of him that way again. However, she had left her high-and-mighty estate and driven all the way downtown to his shop— which wasn't located in the best part of the city. She wouldn't have done that for just any old reason. Plus, judging from the tightness around her mouth, she was seriously riled. And she no doubt planned to aim that riled-ness at him.

Why?

He had a darn good guess. Maybe because he'd shown up at her surprise birthday party? If so, a month was a long time to hold onto that much anger.

But then, this was Natalie.

By the time she stepped inside the shop, all the mechanics and customers had stopped to gawk. It wasn't unwarranted. Natalie was attractive. Not drop-dead gorgeous, either. Her face was much more inter-esting than the surgically perfect socialites who were part of her world. It was an honest face. A face with character. A few tan freckles on her nose. A dimple in her chin.

Natalie had the brains to go with that interesting face, too. Everything she'd done in life was the best. She'd graduated from college with honors, on an athletic scholarship no less. As if that weren't enough, she'd built from the ground up one of the most successful antique shops in the state.

Rick stayed put, gawking at her just as the others were doing. Waiting to see what she wanted. He heard her ask Hal if "the boss" was around, but before Hal could answer, her deep-violety blue eyes slid in his direction. Through the glass, their gazes met. And held.

Natalie didn't even attempt an obligatory smile or offer him a semi-polite nod. Not that he expected it. They were well past the stage of exchanging even fake greetings.

She made her way through the reception area and into the work bay. It was a cemetery of motorcycles and pieces of motorcycles in various stages of repair, disrepair or assembly. Tools, fans and spare parts littered what little floor space there was. The air was heavy not just with heat and humidity but with old oil and gas fumes. Hardly a fitting place for Natalie Sinclair.

He briefly lost sight of her when she meandered around the Harley that he'd just finished, but Rick could hear her heels clicking on the bare cement. And those heel clicks got louder and louder until she appeared in the doorway.

Her gaze landed on him again, and she slid her eyes from his hair, which was still soaking wet, down to his T-shirt. Also drenched. Not just drenched from the water he'd poured over his head, either, but from an ample amount of sweat. If she'd been any other woman, Rick would have wished for a shower and a shave before facing her.

But she wasn't any other woman.

There was no need to impress Natalie. She hated

him. And he felt no love for her, either. In many ways, that made things a lot easier between them. He'd long ago come to terms with their animosity.

Not the attraction though.

"Are you lost?" Rick asked, just so he could make sure his mouth was working.

She stepped inside and slammed the door shut.

Oh, yeah. She was riled.

The stuffed-to-the-brim office was barely big enough for one person, so Rick had to work hard to keep some space between them. He leaned his shoulder against the filing cabinet, folded his arms over his chest and generally tried to appear surly. With the unbearable heat and her impromptu visit, it wasn't a difficult look to achieve.

He hoped.

She stared at him. Nope, it was a glare. And it was a glare through slightly swollen, reddened eyes.

Had she been crying?

Odd. Natalie wasn't a crier.

"I want you to know that I intend to have you arrested," she announced.

Okay. So much for his ploy to be laid back. Her greeting captured Rick's complete attention. "For what? Attending your birthday party?"

Her glare got worse, and her teeth came together. "Attending it wasn't all you did."

He was certain his confused look intensified. "Care to explain that?"

She aimed her index finger at him. "You're the one who needs to explain."

Rick mentally went through any and all of the possibilities, but he didn't come up with one that would warrant this kind of strong reaction.

"Look, we can trade smartass remarks and pointing fingers for hours, but I have a business to run," Rick reminded her. "So, if you're here because you're in a snit about your mother inviting me to the party, then you can get right back in your overpriced car and head home. Because I'm *not* apologizing. Macy begged me to come to your party, and I came as a favor to her. End of story."

Natalie used her fingertips to blot the perspiration from above her upper lip, but she was blotting so hard that Rick was surprised that she wasn't leaving bruises on her skin. "Are you saying nothing out of the ordinary happened that night?"

Rick had already opened his mouth to say you bet nothing happened, but he had to take one giant pause.

Something had happened.

Someone had slipped something into his drink.

His silence seemed to rile her even more, and Natalie flipped open her purse and extracted a small silver handheld DVD player. She deposited it on his desk and pointed to the sole chair in the room. "I think you'll want to sit down for this next part."

"No thanks." That chair would put him even closer to her, and Rick wanted all the distance between them that he could get. "I don't expect this'll take long anyway. I'm not into home movies, and we don't have much to say to each other."

Natalie flexed her eyebrows in a suit-yourself, you'll-regret-it gesture, sat on the edge of his desk next to the DVD player and jabbed the play button. "This is the security film from the night of my party," she explained. Her voice was strained with emotion. "It was taken in the hall just outside my bedroom."

When Rick saw a couple on the small screen, he bit off another surly question about what this could possibly have to do with him. Instead, he concentrated on the images. However, it took him several moments to make out exactly what he was seeing.

Natalie and him.

Or rather it was a couple who *looked* like Natalie and him. Because there was no way it could actually be them.

Not caring for the sickening feeling that suddenly came over him, Rick pushed himself away from the filing cabinet and moved closer to study the images on the screen. "Are you going to tell me why you doctored this video?"

Outrage flashed in her eyes, but she didn't voice it. The rush of emotion seemed to make her queasy. Or maybe it was the sweltering heat. Because she wiped away the perspiration again and slid her hand over her stomach as if to steady it. "I didn't doctor it."

"Then someone did," he fired back.

"Kitt checked," Natalie explained. Her breath was uneven now, and the color was draining from her cheeks. "The images haven't been altered."

"The hell they haven't." Rick watched as the couple got closer and closer to Natalie's bedroom door.

The couple staggered. The woman's right arm banged against the doorjamb. The man didn't fare much better. He crossed in front of her. Staggered as well. And his left shoulder hit against the wall.

That caused Rick's mouth to turn to dust.

The couple's awkward intimate dance continued until the man caught the woman. She went into his arms. Willingly. Their bodies came together. Mouths, too.

In a desperate, hungry kiss.

"I know for a fact that I would have remembered that," Rick insisted in a rough whisper.

Natalie swallowed hard enough that he could hear it. But what she didn't do was agree with him. Instead, she froze the images and pointed to the woman's right arm. "I had a bruise there the morning after my party. I didn't know then how I'd gotten it."

Hell.

Rick waited for the other shoe to fall.

She pointed to the man's left shoulder. To the spot that had rammed into the wall. "Did you have a bruise or any kind of mark?"

Rick didn't even have to think about it. "Yeah. I figured I'd gotten it here at work."

Natalie's posture and bearing were suddenly as unsteady as the couple in the video. "I don't think you got that bruise here."

It took him a moment to get his teeth unclenched so he could speak. "Are you saying you think *that* happened?" Rick asked. "You really believe the two of us had a hot and heavy kissing session outside your bedroom door?"

She closed her eyes. Paused. Gathered her breath. "I don't think the hot and heaviness stopped there. I believe we went inside my bedroom and finished what we started."

Her eyelids lifted, and she met his gaze head-on. "I'm four weeks pregnant. And judging from that video, you're the baby's father."

Chapter Three

"Is this your idea of a bad joke?" Rick asked.

Natalie carefully studied his reaction—his iron jaw, his narrowed gunmetal-gray eyes and thunderstruck expression—and she quickly realized she didn't care for any of it. It was too similar to what her own reaction had been when Kitt first told her about the test results.

She'd expected…what?

A confession?

Perhaps an explanation that would cause all of this to make sense?

Or maybe that's what she hoped he would do, help her make sense of the situation. A miracle of sorts. However, it was obvious Rick didn't have answers or a miracle. Or if he had them, he wasn't ready to share them with her.

That didn't mean he was innocent in all of this.

"*Please* tell me this is a joke," he amended.

"Are you saying you didn't orchestrate what happened?" Natalie countered.

He looked at her as if her ears were on backwards. "You're damn right that's what I'm saying."

And he was adamant about it, too.

Natalie suddenly felt even more desperate, and it was desperation that made her toss the next question at him. "Why should I believe you?"

"Because I'm telling you the truth, that's why." Rick opened his mouth. Closed it. Shook his head. Cursed. "Hell's bells, Natalie, do you really believe I'd drug you so I could sleep with you?"

She'd already asked herself that. At least a dozen times. And during none of that personal questioning had she convinced herself that Rick would do something like this. He wasn't the sort of man who required drugging or any coercion to get a woman into bed.

"I'm pregnant," she restated. "I don't know how it happened, and my only clue is that surveillance video. I need answers, and that's why I'm here."

He shook his head. "What you need is to have the pregnancy test repeated."

"I've already done that." She was up to a dozen times of watching for minus signs on little urine-soaked white plastic sticks. She'd try a dozen more if necessary, praying for one negative result. "They've all been positive."

"Then, you need to see a doctor right away," Rick quickly suggested.

"I did that a few hours ago. I had an ultrasound and a thorough examination. There's definitely a baby."

He cursed again, made his way to the chair, gripped the armrest and dropped down onto the seat. "This can't be happening. The tests, the doctor, the ultrasound and the video are all wrong. They have to be."

She'd had that reaction, too. Denial. It'd taken hours to get past just the tip of it. But she couldn't afford Rick that same amount of time to work through his issues. She had an eerie feeling that time wasn't on their side. "I need you to think back through—"

"Something happened that night," he interrupted. But he didn't say anything else.

Natalie froze. Waited. She forced herself to stay calm. "Obviously something happened," she said when Rick just sat there.

He glanced at her stomach. "I didn't mean *that*. I mean I blacked out."

Her heart had been racing before that, but she could have sworn it stopped mid-beat. Natalie shook her head. "When? How?"

But before he could answer, the phone rang. He waved it off, but the ringing continued and when he perused his shop and apparently realized his employees were all busy, he reached across the desk and answered the phone.

Natalie actually welcomed the interlude. Yes, they needed to get to the bottom of this. Yes, she desperately needed to know what'd happened to her. To them. But she also needed a moment to compose herself. Right now, a thin thread of composure was the only thing that prevented her from screaming. And she didn't want to lose it in front of Rick.

What was going on?

What?

Natalie had been asking herself that for a day and a half and was afraid she wasn't any closer to the truth than she had been when Kitt had first dropped this bombshell.

She was pregnant.

Pregnant!

With a child she couldn't even remember conceiving.

Unplanned motherhood alone would have been more than enough to deal with, but motherhood under these circumstances was terrifying.

"I'll get that work order," she heard Rick say at the end of a heavy, frustrated sigh.

He stood, brushed past her. He was so close that she had no trouble catching his scent. With the nonexistent A/C, the steamy claustrophobic office and the fact that he'd obviously just finished a long day of manual labor, his body odor should have been offensive.

It wasn't.

Far from it.

Oh, there was sweat all right. His white cotton T-shirt was practically soaked, and the snug fabric strained across his toned pecs and arms. His hair was wet as well. His slightly too-long coffee-colored hair fell, permanently disheveled, almost to his shoulders. But he didn't smell sweaty. He somehow managed to smell, well, manly.

He snatched one of the forms from the top of the filing cabinet and read off some figures. Because her energy seemed sapped and her pulse had turned thick and syrupy, Natalie simply sat on the edge of his desk, watching and listening. Waiting for him to finish—without a clue what they would say to each other once he was done. None of her life experiences had prepared her for this.

Rick's movements were jerky. Stiff. Angry. And he kept casting glances her way. Natalie was casting some his way as well.

Sweet heaven, if she thought for one minute that he'd had any voluntary part in this, she would have had him arrested. Except an arrest wouldn't really have given her answers.

Nor would it change what had happened.

She slid her hand over her stomach. A baby. Even though she'd seen the ultrasound, it didn't seem real. Maybe once she understood the circumstances, once she'd heard a plausible explanation—*any* explanation—maybe then she could come to terms with this. It wasn't logical, but at the moment, she needed that hope.

Rick said an abrupt goodbye to the caller and

slammed down the phone as if he'd declared war on it. In the same motion, he waved off one of his employees who was trying to get his attention through the small window.

"What exactly do you remember about that night?" Rick demanded.

The answer was readily available on the tip of her tongue—mainly because she'd already asked herself the same question again and again. "I was on prescription meds, and I was exhausted. So, most of the party is a little blurry."

"How could we not remember *that?*" He pointed to the frozen image of them on the screen.

"I don't know."

He made a sound of agreement. It blended with his jagged huffs of breaths. "How do we know it really happened? Those people could be actors."

"They aren't. Kitt had the images enhanced, and if they're actors, then they're exact replicas of us, right down to my freckles and that little scar on the left side of your neck that you got fly-fishing when you were a kid."

He threw his hands in the air before dropping them to his hips. "Then, maybe that's what they are—actors with very authentic makeup."

She gave a weary been-there-done-that sigh. "I would love it if that were true. But it wouldn't explain the bruise on my arm. Or the bruise on your shoulder. And it certainly wouldn't explain this pregnancy."

"Maybe the pregnancy happened some other time," he fired back.

For some reason, a reason Natalie didn't want to explore, that stung. Yet, Rick certainly had a right to ask that. If their positions had been reversed, she would certainly want to know.

"I haven't had sex in over a year," Natalie explained. Not easily. Discussing her love life—or lack thereof—with Rick Gravari wasn't tops on her list of favorite things to do. "At least, I haven't had sex that I know about."

He cocked his head to the side and gave her a flat look. "And you think you unknowingly had sex with me?"

Weary of the questions and the verbal battle between them, she tipped her head back to the screen. "It's you in that video, Rick. But if you're looking for definitive proof, I don't have it. The video can't be further enhanced. There's no footage from a different angle that might give us a clearer image. And it's too early to do a DNA test to prove paternity. I asked," she added when his flat look was no longer so flat.

That caused a slight lift of his eyebrow. Natalie responded by lifting an eyebrow of her own. And by asking one very important question. "You said you blacked out at the party. What happened?"

He didn't respond right away. Rick groaned softly and scrubbed his hands over his face. "Your caterer, I think."

The fit of temper that Natalie had nourished and fed suddenly cooled. "What does the caterer have to do with any of this?"

"Maybe nothing. Maybe everything." He paused, caught her gaze. "Someone put something in my drink."

Natalie considered what he was saying. "You think that someone was the caterer?"

He nodded. "The only thing I had to eat or drink that night was at your party."

"That proves nothing."

Or did it? Because someone on the catering staff, a man, had given her a drink as well. Sparkling fruit juice. It'd had a somewhat bitter tang to it. At the time Natalie had attributed the taste to her prescription meds.

"No. But the lab test I had done proves *something*," Rick corrected.

That captured Natalie's complete attention. "What lab test?"

There was no sign of cockiness or victory in his stormy gray eyes. There was only frustration and yes, lots of anger and confusion. "When I woke up that morning after the party, I realized I didn't have a clue how I'd gotten home. My motorcycle was there, parked outside the garage, a place I'd never leave it. Never. Since I felt like hell, I went to see my doctor right away. He ran some tests, and the lab found a substance in my blood."

"What kind of substance?" Natalie asked.

Rick shook his head. "It was some kind of narcotic. My doctor had no idea what it was so he sent it out for further testing. The lab is still trying to identify it."

Natalie was so glad she was sitting down. If she hadn't been, that would have sent her in search of a chair. She felt a couple of steps past being light-headed. But she wasn't so light-headed that she didn't immediately spot an inconsistency in his account.

"Why didn't you go to the police with this?" Natalie demanded.

"And tell them what, exactly? That maybe someone at your party slipped an unspecified narcotic into my drink? I decided I'd wait for the lab results before I started pointing any fingers. Of course, that was before I saw that surveillance video. I'm ready to do some finger-pointing now."

Natalie shifted her position slightly, trying to find some kind of equilibrium both mentally and physically. "Why would someone on the catering staff have drugged you?"

"I've asked myself that a dozen times, and the only thing I could come up with was maybe it wasn't intentional. Maybe the beer was contaminated or something."

"Then why wasn't anyone else affected?" she immediately asked.

He stared at her and waited for her to draw her own conclusions. It didn't take long. Rick was likely the only person at the party drinking beer. It was indeed a champagne crowd. But then, she was probably the only one who'd had sparkling fruit juice.

And that in turn meant it would have been fairly easy to drug them.

That explained the *how*, but it certainly didn't explain the *who* and *why*.

"I don't know the caterer," she continued. "And I don't know the man who handed me my drink."

But she could find out, and that's exactly what she intended to do.

Natalie checked her watch. It was nearly 6:00 p.m. and she wished for more hours in the day, because her list of things to do was growing. "I want to talk to your doctor and the lab technician who ran the test on you. I'll also want to talk to my mother, since she's the one who hired the caterer. She'll be home from her therapy session by now. I'll call her."

Rick caught onto her wrist when she reached into her purse for her phone. "Think this through. If you start asking questions about the caterer, your mother will want to know why. And she won't quit until she gets the truth. The *whole truth*. So, if you plan to tell her about the baby tonight, you won't want to do that over the phone."

That was true. Natalie only wished she'd thought of it first.

"We'll drive over there and talk to her," Rick insisted, keeping hold of her wrist.

Natalie shook off his grip. "*We?*"

"*We*," he confirmed. Without warning, he peeled off his damp T-shirt, grabbed a clean one from the bottom drawer of the filing cabinet and slipped it on. "I want to get to the bottom of this, too, and I want as much information as we can get about this caterer."

Natalie almost argued with him. Mainly because it was natural to argue with Rick about any- and everything. But he had a point. The caterer or someone on his or her staff could have orchestrated all of this.

After all, someone had cleaned up the "crime scene."

Someone had gotten both Rick and his motorcycle back to his house. Someone had dressed her for bed and discarded any evidence that anything out of the ordinary had happened. So that meant someone at her party had been involved on a very personal level. Her mother was the first step to figuring out whom.

And they could do that after they told Macy about the pregnancy.

Natalie was already dreading the conversation. It would be messy. Her mother just wasn't very good at handling contingencies, and this pregnancy definitely fell into that category. There'd be tears and perhaps hours of melodrama. Unfortunately, her mother had to know.

Rick grabbed his keys from the desk and headed for the door. Natalie was right behind him.

"We'll take my car," she insisted.

Rick glanced over his shoulder and gave her that look. One she instantly recognized. And hated. She called it his blue-collar/chip-on-the-shoulder glare.

"This has nothing to do with the price of my vehicle," she pointed out. "It's just I'm conveniently parked right out front, and I'm not exactly dressed to climb onto the back of your Harley."

He made a sound to indicate he didn't believe her explanation.

She made a sound to indicate she didn't care what he thought.

It was going to be a long drive to Macy's.

"Besides," she added, "riding a motorcycle in my condition wouldn't be smart. And even you can't argue with that."

He didn't.

With both of them still stewing and no doubt asking themselves a dozen unanswerable questions, Rick let one of his employees know that he needed to run an errand before they got into her car.

Natalie hadn't thought the tension could get any worse, but she was obviously wrong. Without the noise and the distraction of the shop, the silence settled uncomfortably between them. And with each additional moment of silence, Natalie became more and more upset. More and more frightened.

More and more incensed.

Why was this happening?

Why had she become pregnant with Rick's child?

Rick, of all people.

They had so much bad blood between them. Too much. But it hadn't always been that way. Rick and she had known each other since childhood, and her mother had tried to get them together for years. Why, it was never clear to Natalie, but apparently Macy felt that Rick and she were the "perfect couple" destined to lead the "perfect life."

Ironic.

Because her family was old money. To the proverbial manor born. Rick, on the other hand, was a self-made businessman with a keen sense of turning nothing into plenty of something. No Ivy League degree for him. No degree at all. He'd shunned his parents' investment business and had become everything they hadn't wanted him to be—the owner of a custom motorcycle shop. Yet, the normally socially conscious Macy had seemingly overlooked all of that so she could encourage a relationship that Natalie and Rick knew would never happen.

And it wouldn't happen because of that one lapse in judgment three years earlier.

Neither Rick nor she had had much luck coping with that lapse. *Hell on earth* wasn't just a meaningless expression for them. They were living it.

"You're totally certain about this pregnancy?" Rick asked.

Natalie almost preferred the silence to the question. There was none of that chip-on-the-shoulder animosity in his voice, which meant all of this was likely sinking in, and he wasn't taking it too well.

"Dead certain," she assured him.

Rick shook his head, leaned forward. "I don't remember even speaking to you that night."

"Same here," she agreed.

"Yet according to that video, we ended up in the hall outside your bedroom. Kissing. Touching…"

Oh, yes. Definitely kissing. Definitely touching. They'd been all over each other—literally.

Though she knew it wasn't possible, especially since she hadn't remembered anything else, Natalie could have sworn she recalled that kiss.

She glanced at him out of the corner of her eye, and it was as if that one glance opened the hormonal floodgates. There were still no specific memories for the night of the party. But there were other memories, ones that were best forgotten.

As was Rick.

And she'd spent the last three years trying not to remember that he was the most unforgettable man she'd ever known.

It was hard to believe all of his mismatched features could add up to something extraordinary. But heaven help the female population, they did. The olive, bronzy skin: a DNA contribution from his Greek father. Those sizzling gray eyes framed with indecently long lashes. The cheekbones of a Celtic warrior. She'd yet to meet a woman of any age or any background who hadn't found Rick Gravari hot.

Including her.

Much to her disgust.

That one kiss they'd shared three years ago, that one short lapse in judgment had caused someone to die. Not just someone though. Someone they both loved.

"David," she said under her breath.

A little over three years ago David had asked her to marry him. She'd said yes, even though David knew she didn't love him. He also knew she was looking for an out, a way to stop her mother's relentless matchmaking. That's why Natalie had agreed to be his fiancée. But not his wife. She'd told him upfront that there would be no marriage.

David obviously had thought he could change her mind.

Natalie had thought an engagement ring would stop her from wanting Rick. It hadn't. One night, Rick and she had run into each other at a party. They'd talked. Had too much to drink. Had gotten way too close. One thing led to another, and they kissed.

Just as David walked in on them.

Obviously feeling betrayed by his two best friends, David had swallowed what turned out to be a lethal dose of sleeping pills. He'd died in the ER only a few hours later.

David's death would always be with Rick and her. It would always connect them.

And it would always keep them apart.

At least Natalie had been sure of that until now. Until this pregnancy.

She was carrying Rick's baby. That was the one element that neither of them could dismiss. And it was the element that had brought them together.

"Take the next turn to get to Commerce Street," Rick instructed. "And don't put on your blinker."

"Why?" she immediately asked, forcing herself out of her troubling thoughts.

"Just do it."

And for some reason unknown to her, she obeyed him. Maybe it was because she had no fight or argument left in her, but it also had something to do with that suddenly intense expression on Rick's face.

"Do you recognize that SUV behind us?" Rick asked.

Natalie's attention flew to the rearview mirror. There was indeed a black SUV following closely behind them. "No. Why?"

"Because it's been behind us since we left the shop."

"It's probably a coincidence." This particular street wasn't the busiest in the city, but it did lead to several main intersections.

"Maybe." But he didn't sound as if he believed that.

Natalie, on the other hand, decided to hope for the best. She'd already had enough thrown at her for one day without borrowing more trouble.

"Take the next left," Rick told her.

Without turning on her signal, she waited until the last possible second to make the turn. She was going a little too fast, and the tires squealed in protest.

She checked the mirror again.

The SUV made the same slightly out-of-control turn.

Her heart went into overdrive. That turn didn't seem to be a coincidence. It seemed deliberate. But why would someone be following them?

"Speed up," Rick insisted.

Natalie did, and the SUV followed suit. In fact, it continued to mimic her actions when Natalie slowed down and switched lanes.

What the devil was going on?

With that scary question pounding in her head, Natalie slammed her foot on the accelerator and pushed her car well over the speed limit.

The driver of the SUV followed them.

Chapter Four

Rick hadn't thought this day could get any worse.

But he'd obviously thought wrong.

He didn't have a clue why that SUV was following them, but it was. He had no doubts about that. Coupled with the drugged sex/baby news, Rick was ready to concede that he was in the middle of one crazy dream.

Except this was too real to be a dream.

"Turn right," Rick instructed Natalie.

She didn't argue, but he could see the concern all over her face. She was chewing on her bottom lip, and she had a white knuckle death grip on the steering wheel. Still, she made that right turn and sped up. Once again, the SUV stayed right on their bumper.

Both Natalie and he cursed.

"What now?" Natalie asked.

It was too risky to have her stop so he could confront the other driver because Rick had no idea who or what they were dealing with—carjackers, someone with a case of road rage or idiots who'd taken a car out for a joyride. Natalie might be hurt in a confrontation, especially since she probably wouldn't just stay put and let him handle it.

Still, he had to do something.

He pointed to an upcoming intersection. "Take that turn, and drive toward the police station on Arbor Street."

Rick also considered calling the cops, to report what was going on, but he realized he might sound a little paranoid. And he likely was. Besides, if he made the call, there'd be a police report, and he might have to bring up the drugging and the pregnancy. He didn't want to do that yet. Not until they'd spoken to Macy and gotten the information about the caterer.

Natalie took the next turn that would get them to the police station. "What's going on?" she asked. There was more than a tad of desperation in her voice, and though he hadn't thought it possible, she was gripping that steering wheel even harder than before.

Rick didn't mention his theory about road rage or carjackers. Instead, he went with the most benign scenario. "It's probably kids taking their parents' car for a joyride."

But he couldn't discount that this was yet another incident of unnerving things that just didn't make sense. First, someone had drugged them. From the looks of that video, it'd been a date-rape-type drug.

Or maybe some weird, powerful aphrodisiac that'd induced memory loss.

And why?

So that Natalie and he would head to her bedroom and therefore place themselves in a compromising position?

Was that it?

Had this really been some sort of elaborate blackmail or revenge scheme? Had someone taken pictures of them having sex and was that person planning to use them in some sinister way?

He gave that some thought and decided that didn't make sense, either.

Nothing about this made sense.

Neither Natalie nor he was married. Nor were either involved in a relationship. It was the same for their jobs. Their businesses wouldn't be adversely affected if their customers learned they'd had sex.

So, what could possibly be the point?

Rick didn't have an answer for that, either.

Frustrated and concerned, he checked the side mirror again and didn't think it was his imagination that the SUV was even closer. He considered having Natalie slam on her brakes, which would almost certainly cause a rear-end collision. That would allow him to get a good look at whoever was following them, but it would also put Natalie at risk.

And perhaps the baby.

Not only did he have to consider Natalie's safety, but they both had to consider the child.

"We should be at the police station in about five minutes," Rick let Natalie know. He'd hoped that would relieve some of the tension in her body. It didn't.

Instead, her eyes widened.

Rick's attention went back to the mirror. The SUV had sped up again. And it was no longer behind them. It'd moved out into the lane to the left of them. It pulled up, driving until the two vehicles were side by side.

"Can you see who's behind the wheel?" Natalie asked. She glanced over at the SUV just for a second.

Rick tried and failed to see who was inside. "The windows are too heavily tinted. Just keep driving and try to stay calm. Nothing's going to happen. It's still broad daylight, and there are three other cars nearby."

However, high visibility apparently wasn't enough to deter the SUV driver.

The vehicle swerved to the right, moving directly into their lane. Natalie veered to avoid it, but the SUV immediately repeated the maneuver. That wasn't the action of a bad driver. Or a joyrider.

This person was trying to run them off the road.

Rick caught onto the steering wheel so he could help Natalie maintain control of her car. He kept watch on the front end of the SUV, and every time it made a move toward them, Rick and Natalie moved her car out of the way.

"We're going into the emergency lane," Rick explained just seconds before he steered the vehicle in that direction. "Hit the brakes now."

She did, and instantly there was the sound of tires screeching on the hot asphalt. The SUV apparently hadn't expected them to do that because it sped on ahead.

Rick saw the other vehicle's brake lights, but it was too late to try to cut into the emergency lane and back up. There were cars coming directly behind them. The SUV had to speed up to keep from being hit.

Rick held his breath until the other vehicle was out of sight. "Are you okay?" he asked Natalie.

"No. I'm not." She groaned, and Rick pried her hands off the steering wheel so that she wouldn't have bruises. "What is going on?"

"I don't know."

She smacked her hand on the steering wheel. "Do you think this is all connected to the pregnancy?"

"No," he answered.

And he hoped that was true.

But Rick had a nasty feeling in the pit of his stomach that the driver of that SUV had wanted to harm them.

"I fired a mechanic about two weeks ago," Rick said. He kept a close watch on the cars speeding past them. He wanted to make sure that SUV didn't do a turnaround and come right back at them. "Maybe the guy was more riled than I thought he was."

Natalie nodded and she seemed to calm a little. "I had to let someone go, too. A housekeeper. About a month ago. Because she was stealing things." She paused. "That might explain who was in that SUV, but even a pair of disgruntled former employees probably wouldn't have come up with a plan to punish us with drugs and a pregnancy. It'd be easier just to hurt us. Or kill us."

Rick was on the same page with her. But that didn't mean there weren't answers out there.

"Macy," he mumbled.

Natalie repeated her mother's name under her breath. "Give me a few minutes to compose myself, and then let's have that chat with her."

Definitely.

And he prayed that Macy would have answers.

"You won't be able to see your mother this evening. She's had a difficult day, and I don't want her disturbed."

Natalie stared at her mother's personal assistant, Troy Jackson, as he delivered his message. Troy, the blond, blue-eyed, beefcake pretty boy, was doing his best to block the front door so that Natalie and Rick couldn't enter.

No amount of blocking would work this evening. Rick rolled his eyes and just muscled Troy aside.

Troy might have a weightlifter's body, but Natalie figured he was essentially a wimp and wouldn't attempt to take on Rick. She didn't blame Troy. With

Rick's fierce expression and don't-mess-with-me demeanor, it was clear he meant business.

So did she.

Natalie was tired of having lost control over her life. She was tired of having things happen that didn't make sense. She was especially tired of not having a logical explanation for what had happened. Only after Rick and she got that explanation would they be able to figure out what their course of action might be.

"You tell Macy that we have to speak to her," Rick called out as Troy barreled up the stairs— probably to tattle to Macy that they'd barged their way in. "If she's too tired or upset to come down, we're coming up. Because one way or another, we're talking to her tonight."

Rick was obviously so furious that Natalie considered trying to calm him down. But she wasn't in a calming-down sort of mood herself. She was pregnant, and someone either wanted to scare her, torment her or kill her. And it was entirely possible her mother could give them some clues as to why this was happening.

Nope.

There'd be no calming down, and this conversation was going to take place.

"Are you sure you're up to this?" Rick asked.

She glanced at him and saw that he was watching her. Studying her, really. Probably because she didn't look too steady. "Trust me, I'm up to it."

"Because if you're not, I can do this alone." His attention drifted down to her stomach.

Oh.

She understood then.

Rick was questioning her *delicate condition*. Not a bad term for it, either. She did feel delicate. Fragile. Dazed. And confused. But fortunately, the need for answers outweighed the early symptoms of pregnancy and the adrenaline fatigue caused by the incident with the SUV.

"I could do this alone as well," she countered.

But the sudden steel in Rick's jaw let her know that he was staying put.

That didn't surprise her. Rick was the sort of take-charge man who was rock-solid in a crisis. He would indeed stay put and stand by her.

For how long though?

That was a sobering question. Natalie would have preferred someone else's help—anyone else's—but she had to admit that Rick had a vested interest in this.

He was the baby's father.

Just thinking about that little fact caused Natalie's stomach to sink. Fate certainly had a strange sense of humor.

"You need to sit down," she heard Rick insist. But he didn't just insist, he caught onto her arm and led her into the adjacent living room.

Natalie nearly protested the kid-glove treatment, but she quickly realized it was necessary. She was indeed dizzy, and Rick had no doubt noticed that she wasn't too steady on her feet. He plopped her down on the sofa and went to the bar to pour her a glass of water.

She took the water from him, meeting his gaze over the top of the cut-crystal glass. "Thank you."

Before Natalie said that last part, he'd looked ready for battle, but the steel in his jaw softened a bit, and after a heavy sigh, he eased down on the granite coffee table across from her. "I don't want you to worry," he said. "I'll get to the bottom of this."

She believed him. However, Natalie believed in her abilities as well. *They* would get to the bottom of it. But that wouldn't change one vital point.

"No matter who's responsible, I'm still four weeks pregnant."

"I know." He groaned and scrubbed his hand over his face. "I can't go back and change that. Sorry."

He was sincere. Natalie didn't doubt that. She also didn't doubt that this was as much of a life-changing experience for him as it was for her. Which led her to the next question.

What were they going to do about the baby?

It wasn't as if they were a couple. They could barely tolerate being in the same room with each other.

Well, that wasn't exactly true at the moment.

They were in the same room together. On the same side, so to speak. With a huge shared concern.

Their baby.

Even though she couldn't recall the sex that had

created the child, the pregnancy itself created a new sort of intimacy between them. An intimacy that she was certain neither of them was prepared to deal with.

"What are the odds?" Rick asked. He didn't wait for her to ask what he meant. "That we'd have drugged sex at the very time you'd be ovulating?"

Natalie had already been through this during her frantic pregnancy tests and trips to the doctor. Unfortunately, that little detail only made all of this seem more sinister. Had someone planned that, too? Other than herself, there weren't a lot of people who knew about the timing of her menstrual cycle. Kitt, maybe.

Perhaps even Macy.

Rick opened his mouth. Closed it. And it seemed as if he changed his mind a dozen times about what he wanted to say. "Will you, uh, keep the baby?"

"Yes." Natalie answered so quickly that he probably believed she'd given it no thought. She had. Plenty of it. "Call it my personal beliefs, whatever, but this child is mine… *Ours*," she corrected. "I'll definitely keep it."

Though that *ours* had not come easily.

It might take her a lifetime to begin to feel comfortable including Rick in any part of her life. Still, that discomfort didn't extend to the baby. Now that she was beginning to come to terms with the fact that she was indeed pregnant, she had also come to realize that she would love this child no matter how it had been conceived.

Rick nodded, but she couldn't tell if that was a nod of approval or if he simply didn't know how else to react. She didn't have time to ask because Natalie heard footsteps. Macy's footsteps, no doubt. Caused by a pair of ridiculously high spike heels coming down the staircase.

Natalie set her water glass aside and watched her mother make her way from the foyer and into the room. Macy didn't seem too steady on her feet, perhaps because of the heels. The footwear complimented her outfit: a short, slim lipstick-red dress that would have been more appropriate for a college student on a date than for a fifty-two-year-old woman. Not that Macy looked her age. Far from it. Of course, at least a half dozen cosmetic surgeries and a pampered lifestyle were responsible for that.

"Rick. Natalie," Macy greeted. But it wasn't much of a greeting. As Macy walked closer, Natalie could see that her mother's eyes were red, and her mascara was smeared as if she'd been crying. The extra proof of that was the wadded-up handkerchief she held in her right hand.

"I know why you're here," Macy said. "I know that you're pregnant." She slowly walked to the chair. Sighing deeply, she sank down on the cushion, and she made eye contact with Natalie. "Your sister dropped by about an hour ago and let me know what was going on."

Natalie should have anticipated that her sister

would do that. Kitt was looking out for her. And Kitt was also probably trying to prepare her mother for the shocking news. Judging from her mother's teary eyes and shaken demeanor, Macy was already on her way to coping. Which was good. Because unfortunately, Rick and she were going to have to press Macy for information.

Macy leaned back against the chair, and Natalie could see that her mother's perfectly manicured fingers were trembling. "Kitt said you believe you were drugged the night of your birthday party?"

"We were," Rick verified, his tone tense but somehow still respectful. "I had lab tests done so I have proof of that."

"So it's true." Macy shook her head and swiped at another tear. "I'd prayed it wasn't true."

Rick reached over and gently put his hand over hers. "Macy, what do you know about the caterer you hired for Natalie's party?"

Macy reacted with a sharp gasp, and her eyes widened. "Oh, God. You don't think…" But she didn't finish it. She ended with another "Oh, God."

"We don't know what to think at this point, but we need the name of the caterer," Rick pressed. "It's important that we ask him or her some questions."

"Of course." Macy nodded. "It's Antoine Dupree, but I don't think he did the work himself. I remember him saying he was going to have to subcontract because he was busy with a wedding."

That was not what Natalie wanted to hear. If the caterer had indeed hired out the work, then it would be another level to dig through to come up with names of possible suspects. It also wouldn't help if there'd been a huge staff. She couldn't remember a lot about her own party, but Natalie figured there were at least a half-dozen people working.

Any one of them could have been responsible.

"We know the caterer or someone on his staff would have had the opportunity to put a drug into the food or drinks," Rick continued. "But what we don't know is why someone would do this. There have been no blackmail attempts. And judging from the surveillance tapes, no one entered Natalie's bedroom to take incriminating photos of us. That leaves us with no motive for this crime."

"Did the surveillance tapes show you leaving Natalie's bedroom?" Macy asked. "Or the better question would be—did it show anyone taking you out of there?"

Rick shook his head. "Someone or something jammed the surveillance feed."

"Kitt said it wouldn't be that hard to do," Natalie added. "But that means the person would have known in advance about the security system. In other words, they would have had to bring the jamming equipment with them. Coupled with the drugging, that makes it premeditated."

When Macy didn't respond, Natalie asked what

both Rick and she needed to know. "Can you think of any reason why the caterer or someone on his staff would want to do this to us?"

"I can think of a reason. A *bad* reason." Her voice broke, and Macy stood slowly and made her way to the window. "God help me. I should have told you sooner."

Natalie froze. She'd wanted to hear her mother's denial. *Any* denial. However, this didn't sound like the start of something like that.

"I'm not really sure if this is all connected. But maybe it is…" Macy turned and faced them. "Your father and I and Rick's parents were all friends at university together, and we became involved in eugenics research. Specifically, we became involved with the Cyrene Project."

Natalie repeated those last two words under her breath. It wasn't the first time she'd heard them. No. As a child, she'd heard her parents say them.

In whispers, sometimes.

Other times, the words had been parts of rather loud arguments.

In fact, Natalie had heard her father mention the Cyrene Project the day he walked out and left his family when she was barely six years old. His leaving had preceded a very bitter divorce. It'd continued to be bitter until her father's accidental death when she was seventeen.

"The Cyrene Project?" Rick commented, sounding very skeptical and not at all pleased with the topic. "What does this have to do with the drugging?"

"Maybe everything," Macy said softly. Not her usual drama-queen level of emotion, either. Her voice was small and thin. "The Cyrene Project was an experiment to produce genetically superior babies."

Natalie had speculated as to what the project was, but she hadn't even come close in her conjecture.

She stared at her mother and tried to process what she'd just heard.

She couldn't.

Natalie glanced at Rick, but he didn't appear to understand this any more than she did. Her mother had been having episodes of odd behavior, and Natalie couldn't help but wonder if she was having one now.

"Your father and I were paired because our DNA was compatible," Macy continued a moment later. "That's why we married. That's why we had children."

Rick cursed again. "Macy, you're not making any sense."

"I'm making perfect sense," Macy insisted. "And I'm telling you the truth. Your parents were paired as well, even though they weren't a couple before. Did you know that your mother was dating your uncle Carlton until the Cyrene Project?"

Rick shrugged. "I knew they'd dated." He said it in a matter-of-fact tone, but Natalie could see that he was trying to piece all of this together. So was she.

"Your mother agreed to marry your father because

he was the most suitable DNA candidate," Macy insisted. "We wanted superior babies through eugenic matching, and that's exactly what we got. All of you, including Natalie's brother and sister, are superior in every way."

Superior.

Yes, that was true. All four of them had higher-than-average intelligence. All had been better-than-average athletes. Natalie hadn't really considered that before, but she considered it now.

"All right," Rick said. He aimed his index finger at Macy. Lowered it. And he started to pace. "For argument's sake, let's say this project existed. Actually, it'd explain a lot because heaven knows there wasn't much love in my parents' marriage. It was the same for you, Macy. I could see that even though I was just a kid. But what does the Cyrene Project have to do with anything that happened to Natalie and me?"

Macy swallowed hard and lowered her head. "It has everything to do with you. *Everything*. It's because of the Cyrene Project that Natalie's pregnant."

Chapter Five

To put it mildly, Macy's revelation floored him.

Rick stopped pacing, and his hands went on his hips. He stared at Macy waiting for more of the explanation. When it didn't come, he asked, "You're saying this Cyrene Project is responsible?"

"Yes." Macy walked to the bar, poured herself a shot of Kentucky bourbon and downed it in one gulp. It took a few deep breaths and a headshake to deal with the straight liquor which had no doubt burned her throat and watered her eyes. "Before you were even born, you two were already paired for the second phase of the project."

Rick didn't know whether to continue cursing or to laugh. Judging from Natalie's expression, she was trying to make the same decision.

This just kept getting crazier and crazier. Which made him wonder—had Macy gone insane? Except she seemed not insane, but adamant.

"That's the reason I wanted the two of you together when you were younger," Macy continued. She set the empty glass back on the bar, poured a second shot and drained the liquid. "That's the reason I pushed so hard with the matchmaking. Not any more though. *Not any more*."

"Hell," Rick mumbled.

Natalie mumbled something similar, and they waited for her mother to continue.

"To the day I die, I'll regret that I ever got involved with the Cyrene Project," Macy said. "Because of it, I married a man I didn't love. A man who didn't love me. And yes, we had three beautiful, intelligent children, but for years I've had to live with the fact that I cheated Mother Nature. I don't think Mother Nature likes it when people do that. She's punishing me. That's why I have these horrible headaches. That's why I can't sleep, why I hear these voices."

Rick held up his hand to stop her from saying more about nature's wrath. He already had enough information spinning in his head, and he'd reached maximum overload. There was a bottom line here, *somewhere*, and he wanted to get to it now. Later he'd need to deal with Macy's obvious health problems. Something would have to be done.

"Just answer this—did someone associated with the Cyrene Project drug us?" he asked Macy.

Macy reached for another drink, but Rick got up

and stopped her. She might need the bourbon to get through this, but he wanted her sober for the rest of this explanation. He only hoped the next part made more sense than the first.

But he wasn't counting on it.

At the moment, little about his life made sense.

Rick caught onto Macy's shoulders, spun her around and forced her to face him. Natalie quickly joined him. Side by side.

"Who. Drugged. Us?" Natalie demanded, clearly frustrated with her mother's account.

Tears filled Macy's eyes, and she frantically shook her head. "I think it might have been Dr. Benjamin."

Whoa. Rick hadn't expected that answer. Not even close. Obviously, neither had Natalie. She actually dropped back a step, and the color drained from her cheeks.

"Our family doctor?" Natalie asked, the disbelief and the shock straining her voice.

Rick knew exactly how she felt because Dr. Benjamin had been his physician until he'd moved closer to his motorcycle shop. And not once had he suspected the doctor of some plot to improve the DNA of the human race.

"Dr. Benjamin started the Cyrene Project a little over thirty years ago," Macy explained. "Rick, you were his first successful offspring. Natalie came a few months later. Then, Wyatt and Kitt."

Rick let go of Macy so he could catch onto

Natalie—who suddenly looked woozy. She didn't resist his attempt to steady her.

"I can't believe this," Natalie mumbled.

Rick had her sit on a bar stool so he could continue this interrogation of her mother. And, yep, it had become an interrogation. He only hoped he could get any information that would help them. Macy was obviously hanging by a thin emotional thread.

"How did Dr. Benjamin drug us?" Rick asked.

Macy directed her answer to Natalie. "Remember, you'd been to Dr. Benjamin's office right before you came home for the party?"

Natalie nodded. "Yes. He gave me prescription meds, and they made me drowsy." She paused and swallowed hard. "He's the one who confirmed the pregnancy."

Oh, man.

Rick didn't like the way the pieces of this puzzle were coming together.

Groaning, Natalie squeezed her eyes shut for a moment. When she opened them, there was no more wooziness. There was fire in the depths of all those shades of blue. "Mother, why in the name of heaven didn't you tell us this sooner?"

"I…well…" Macy fumbled with her words a moment longer before she cleared her throat and continued. "Because I didn't really think Dr. Benjamin would go through with his plan."

"And you're positive he did?" Rick asked.

"Who else could it have been? Dr. Benjamin and I had a huge argument about this the day of your party. I told him to stay away from you." Macy tried to pour herself another drink, but once again Rick stopped her. She stared into his eyes. "I didn't tell you sooner because I thought it would go away. I thought the promises we made all those years ago were long forgotten."

"What promises?" Rick and Natalie asked in unison.

Macy hesitated a moment and then snapped her fingers as if remembering something important. "I have papers," she said. "I'll get them." And with that, she hurried across the room and to the stairs.

Rick considered following her but dismissed that idea when he noticed Natalie had even less color in her face than she'd had when they'd started this conversation with her mother. He'd known Natalie all her life, and he'd rarely seen her upset, much less shaken to the core.

But he was seeing it now.

"This is a nightmare," she whispered.

Rick walked closer to her, just in case Natalie needed him. He was more than a little concerned about her present well-being. She was facing a totally unexpected pregnancy and her life had recently been endangered. That was too much stress for one person to deal with. Oh, yeah. And there was the whole dilemma of what to do about a mother who'd been lying her entire life.

Of course, his own parents had doled out the same lies.

Too bad they weren't alive so he could confront them. Because heaven knew he needed to hold someone accountable for this.

"What kind of papers could possibly cause this to make sense?" Natalie asked.

Rick shook his head. "I don't know about making sense, but Macy might have some evidence against Dr. Benjamin."

"Yes. Maybe he put his plans in writing and gave Macy a copy." She paused, obviously considering that and nodded. "I can't believe Dr. Benjamin would do something like this. I can't believe I trusted him."

Natalie didn't start to tremble, and she no longer seemed on the verge of falling apart because of the stress. She did exactly what Rick figured she would do. She hiked up her chin and took a deep breath as if preparing herself for the huge task ahead of her.

That act would have fooled most people.

Not him though.

She was still fighting hard to maintain control. However, this was a losing battle. It was a lost battle for him as well. The emotion, the adrenaline, the confusion and the anger all whipped together until it just felt overwhelming.

"Maybe this is some cosmic form of punishment," she whispered.

Yeah. Because of David. Rick had already played

around with the idea, and he'd dismissed it. "The cosmos has better things to do than come after us. I'm betting that whatever happened is of a human origin with a means, motive and opportunity."

"Dr. Benjamin," she supplied. And with that, he noticed her bottom lip trembling. She was slowly losing that tentative chokehold she had on her emotions.

That tremble was more than Rick could handle. Knowing it was a mistake and not caring, he reached out and pulled her into his arms. She went willingly, fitting against him as if she belonged there.

He quickly shoved that last thought aside.

"If Benjamin is behind this, we'll press charges," he promised. Though Rick didn't have a clue what crimes the man had actually committed.

"*If* we can prove he did it," Natalie challenged.

"Oh, we'll prove it all right. We'll have my lab-test results and your surveillance video. That, along with what your mother told us will be more than enough for the police to launch an investigation into Dr. Benjamin's baby project."

She lowered her head until it almost touched his shoulder. "But even if he's arrested, he's still succeeded. He's created a phase-two baby, and I'm carrying it."

True. And there was no getting around that. They were well on their way to becoming parents—a truly humbling and frightening thought.

There were times, like now, when he wondered if he could ever come to terms with it.

"We'll work everything out," he assured her. Rick pulled her deeper into his embrace. Not just because she needed it. But because he needed her to be in his arms.

Natalie froze. Looked up at him. And she went completely stiff.

There was a moment, hardly more than a few seconds, when their gazes met. Their breaths met.

Rick didn't have a name or label for it, but they connected on a level where they shouldn't be connected.

It was still there. The energy. The flicker of attraction. Except it didn't feel as small as a flicker right now. It felt more like a blazing flame that radiated from the center of his body.

Not good.

Because he knew for a fact that particular part of him rarely made wise decisions.

"We can't," Natalie said, pulling away. Gone was the tremble, the vulnerability. Natalie was back. "I can't."

"It was just a hug. It didn't mean anything."

But they both knew what'd happened the last time they'd gotten this close. Well, knowingly this close. Obviously, since Natalie was pregnant, they'd gotten a lot closer and a lot more intimate.

Before Rick could stop them, a few erotic images went through his head. Images of Natalie and him naked, having sex. Good images.

And bad ones.

Since those bad ones were giving him equally bad thoughts, Rick stepped back both mentally and physically.

Natalie was right. They couldn't do this. Hugs for comfort, or any other kinds of hugs, would just be playing with fire. They couldn't afford this dangerous game.

She picked up her water and drank some. "I'm scared. And I hate having to admit I'm scared—especially to you. I'm also furious. And upset. And, God, I'm dizzy."

The outburst seemed to drain her, and she leaned against the bar.

"The dizziness is probably part of the pregnancy," Rick assured her in the calmest voice he could muster. "I remember hearing it takes a while for a woman's body to adjust to the hormone surges."

"Surges, huh?" she mumbled, sounding a little relieved. And annoyed. She frowned at him. "Don't go all understanding on me. It'd only confuse me at a time when I don't need any more confusion. And it'd hurt your bad-boy image."

He smiled. He couldn't help it. "To heck with the image. I'm in this with you."

"And that's supposed to make me feel better?" But Natalie waved him off. "Sorry. I didn't mean that as witchy as it sounded."

That put a quick end to any smiling. "I know what you meant." He deserved it. He deserved worse. "But we have to put aside what happened with David. We need to work through this together."

She hesitated. Then nodded. "Because we don't know what we're dealing with." Natalie put her water aside and folded her arms over her chest. "I heard my parents argue about the Cyrene Project. I had no idea it had anything to do with me, Kitt and my brother."

At least he was an only child and was therefore the only one in his family affected. But Rick had to wonder—was this Cyrene Project limited just to the four of them? Or had other students and doctors been involved? And if so, had any of them experienced this premeditated paternity?

Just how far did this grand scheme go?

He played around with that question for a moment, until it brought him back full circle to what'd happened on their way to Macy's.

"The SUV doesn't fit into any of this," Rick said, thinking aloud. "If Dr. Benjamin went through all of this to make sure we produced a baby, then he wouldn't have sent someone to try to hurt us."

"You're right." She sat up straighter in the chair. "So, maybe we can dismiss that as a coincidence."

Rick hoped that was true. They already had enough to deal with.

"But I can't dismiss my mother's symptoms." Natalie got up, walked across the room and picked up the phone. "She's having headaches and hearing voices."

"What are you doing?" Rick asked.

"I want to call a friend who's a psychiatrist. I'll make an appointment for my mother."

It was a good idea, and it would give Macy some psychological support to get through this.

"When we're done here, I'll pay Dr. Benjamin a visit," Rick told her.

Natalie angled her eyes in his direction. "Not without me you won't. He has some explaining to do, and I want to hear what he has to say."

Yes, and once the doctor was done explaining, Rick was calling the cops. He only hoped Dr. Benjamin wouldn't become violent when they confronted him. Of course, as Natalie had pointed out, the doctor wouldn't want to hurt them now that he'd successfully ensured the conception of the baby.

At least he wouldn't want to hurt Natalie.

As the baby's father, he was now expendable.

Rick decided it would be a good idea to take a weapon with him. Just in case. While he was at it, he'd also try to talk Natalie into staying as far away from Dr. Benjamin as she could stay. Of course, Rick knew he had little or no chance of convincing Natalie to do that. She wanted to confront the man who'd turned her life upside down, and Rick couldn't blame her. He planned to do some confronting as well.

While Natalie was on the phone with her doctor friend, Rick used his cell to call his own doctor, Eric

Macomb. The police would no doubt need his lab results to prove that he'd been drugged.

And that brought on a troubling thought.

Natalie had been drugged, too, and he didn't know how something like that would affect the baby. Of course, there had been no baby while the drug had been at a high level in her body. Plus, if all of this went back to Dr. Benjamin—if he was indeed the culprit behind everything—he wouldn't have used a harmful drug and risk any damage to the baby.

Dr. Macomb's nurse answered, and she put Rick on hold so she could check on the lab results. Less than a minute later, she came back on the line with news that Rick didn't want to hear.

The results weren't ready yet.

Frustrated, Rick emphasized to her how important that particular lab work was, and he left a message for Dr. Macomb to call him ASAP.

Because Natalie was speaking practically in a whisper to the doctor, Rick had no trouble hearing Macy's shoes click their way across the foyer and toward them. She appeared in the entryway.

With no visible papers in her hands.

And she was smiling.

"Natalie. Rick," Macy greeted, waltzing back into the room. "You two look frazzled. As I probably do. I wasn't expecting guests tonight."

Rick couldn't have been more surprised if she'd slapped him. "Are you all right?" he asked Macy.

Natalie was obviously concerned as well because she quickly ended her call and stood. "Mom?"

Macy smiled again and shook her head. "Why wouldn't I be all right?"

Rick and Natalie exchanged a disquieting glance.

"Macy, you were supposed to be getting some papers," Rick reminded her.

"Papers?" Macy shrugged. "I have no idea what you're talking about."

Chapter Six

"I don't need to rest," Natalie insisted, but she might as well have been talking to the air. Because Rick was parking in front of her house anyway despite her protest. "What I need is to find Dr. Benjamin."

"We've already tried. We called all over the city, and we can't find him. It's getting late, and there's nothing else we can do tonight."

Rick used *that* tone. The one that set her teeth on edge. The me-Tarzan, you-Jane tone that let her know that he believed he was in charge here.

If Natalie hadn't been so exhausted, she would have put up more of a fight. But she *was* exhausted. And Rick was correct in this case. It would be a waste of time to drive all over the city looking for the doctor, especially since his answering service had informed them that he'd be at his office the following day.

"We'll get a good night's sleep and talk to the SOB first thing in the morning," Rick added.

Natalie cleared her throat to indicate she wasn't buying that good night's sleep part.

He shrugged. "Okay, so you'll *try* to sleep. For the sake of the baby."

Until Rick had tacked on that last part, Natalie had been ready to argue with him again. But he was right about that as well.

Damn him.

He followed her inside, and as she pressed in the numbers on the keypad to stop the whine of her security system, Rick immediately began to look around. And that sent her heartbeat racing again.

"You don't think someone broke in?" she asked.

"No. I'm just checking." He did, too. Rick made his way through the house, opening doors and looking inside the rooms. "Is Kitt coming back tonight?" he called out to her from the top of the stairs.

"No. When I phoned her about an hour ago, she said she was going to spend the night with Macy." Considering how Macy was acting, that was a necessity. "She also wanted to look around for those mysterious papers."

If they existed.

Natalie was afraid the papers might be a figment of her mother's odd behavior. That was yet something else for her to worry about. She'd be on pins and needles until they had the results back from the medical exam, and that wouldn't happen until morning.

"Where are all your servants?" Rick asked.

That riled her a bit, too, mainly because his question made it seem as if she had employees who waited on her hand and foot. Of course, Natalie had to concede that he might simply want information as to who might be around, so she tried to sound civil when she responded.

"The housekeeper and the cook aren't live-ins. They left hours ago. Since tomorrow is Sunday and they have the day off, neither of them will be back in until day after tomorrow."

He mumbled something under his breath and resumed his search. The mumble had probably been because he'd just realized they were alone.

Natalie did some mumbling of her own.

"Remember, I do have a security system," she pointed out, making her way up the stairs. "And Kitt installed some kind of device that'll make it harder to jam."

She only hoped it would work better than it had last time.

"The system covers all the windows and doors?" Rick asked.

"Yes." She went down the hall toward the sound of his voice so she could explain that according to Kitt, it was the best security system money could buy, but Rick came out of one of the guest rooms and ran right into her.

Literally.

Body against body.

He was solid. All muscle and strength. He reached out, temporarily scooping her into his arms, probably to make sure she wasn't off-balance. The embrace lasted mere seconds before he stepped away.

Natalie immediately felt the loss of his arms, the warmth and strength of his body. And she hated that it felt like a loss. She shouldn't be thinking about Rick's arms.

Or any other part of him.

Especially the parts that involved kissing and sex.

What was wrong with her anyway? She had more than enough problems without having sex dreams about Rick Gravari.

"Everything seems clear," he informed her. He glanced around the hall, looking at everything but her. An indication that the embrace had had some kind of effect on him, too.

Mercy.

Something was wrong with both of them.

"I'll get you something to eat." He stepped around her. "Then you should get some rest."

Natalie shook her head and latched onto his arm so he couldn't leave. It was time to get something straight. "Rick, you don't have to play nursemaid, chef or bodyguard. I'm more than capable of taking care of myself. Last I heard, pregnancy doesn't equal helplessness."

He shifted, and that slight shift put him closer to her. He stared at her. "Let's get something straight.

You hate me. I know that. But you're just going to have to set that hatred aside and let me help you, understand? Because we don't know what we're dealing with. You could be in danger. The baby could be in danger."

Oh. So, the baby was his bottom-line motivation. Especially, keeping the baby safe. She didn't approve of his ultimatum. No surprise there. But Natalie couldn't fault his reasoning or his concern.

She finally nodded.

Why?

Because the man was batting a thousand in the being-right department.

Still, Natalie had to make sure he knew that this pregnancy would not make her a wimp. Nothing could do that. "I won't let you take over my life."

Which, of course, sounded petty in the grand scheme of things. Still, she wanted some boundaries. Some barriers. Especially since the ones they'd spent years erecting were tumbling down around them.

"I don't want to take over your life," Rick assured her. "But I will protect you. I might be the last person on earth you want as the father of your child, but I do have a few attributes that might come in handy in this situation. I can kick some serious ass if necessary."

Rick definitely fell into the alpha male, butt-kicking category. Ironic. She'd never really considered that an asset. Appealing, yes. Arousing, too.

But never an asset.

Until now.

If it came down to it, Rick would protect her. Because she was carrying his child. And that made him a very good person to have on her side right now.

Even if it complicated the heck out of her already complicated life.

Rick walked to the end of the hall and stopped just outside her bedroom door. He propped his hands on his hips, looked around, and his attention finally landed on the tiny cherub sconce mounted on the corner wall. That small decorative piece hid the equally small security camera. The one that'd captured the beginning of their drugged sexual encounter.

Natalie tipped her head to the camera. "Kitt hid it that way because she thought we had a problem with a former maid stealing things."

Thank goodness, too. Without the camera, Natalie wouldn't have known who the father of her baby was. Of course, she also wouldn't have had such vivid images of being in Rick's arms. It was a double-edged sword.

"I want to remember what happened that night," she heard him say.

"Excuse me?" Natalie walked closer, certain she'd misunderstood him.

Rick turned, looked at her. "I want to remember who drugged us," he clarified.

"Oh." And she felt the blush warm her cheeks. Despite her earlier self-admonishment, her mind still wasn't where it should be because she'd immediately thought that he wanted to recall what had happened in the bedroom.

Unfortunately, Natalie had been thinking a lot about that particular bedroom activity, and her imagination was working overtime. It didn't help that she'd often fantasized about Rick. A lot.

Before David's death, anyway.

However, since then Natalie had managed to bury those fantasies. And she would continue to do just that. The only way she could deal with the guilt of David's death was to keep the one promise he'd asked of Rick and her—to stay away from each other.

And they would.

Bolstered by her mental lecture, Natalie opened her bedroom door. "I'll get some rest. You do the same."

But Rick didn't nod or agree; he just stood there. "I'm not leaving this house."

Yes. She'd already figured that out. He was still in the me-Tarzan mode, and it would take too much energy to convince him otherwise. Besides, she really didn't want to spend the night alone in the house. Even Rick's presence was preferable to that.

"You can stay in the guest room," she offered.

Natalie almost slipped into perfect-hostess mode and offered to locate him pajamas or something, but that only stirred a thought that Rick probably wasn't the type. She would bet her favorite antique Irish sideboard that he slept bare-butt naked.

Oh, that conjured up yet another unwanted image.

Rick, naked on her pearl-colored Egyptian cotton sheets.

"Are you okay?" he asked.

Since Natalie had no idea what had prompted that question, and since she was having a lot of trouble focusing, she just waited for him to explain.

"You were staring at me."

Ah. So she was. "I'm exhausted," she said as if that clarified everything.

He flexed his eyebrows, and she wanted to wince. It was hard to BS a man like Rick.

"One way or another, even if it drives us crazy," he said turning away from her and heading toward the guest room, "we'll get through this."

It sounded like a promise, but Natalie had no idea how he could keep it. The only thing they could possibly do was work to solve the riddle of what'd happened to them. Once they had the culprit identified and behind bars, then they could begin to deal with everything else.

"I don't hate you, Rick," she told him. Why, she didn't know. Maybe because after all his help, she felt guilty about the animosity between them.

He stopped. Didn't move. He just stood there with his back to her. "I don't hate you, either." Rick turned slightly and looked at her over his shoulder. "But that's not necessarily a good thing."

With that, he went into the guest room. Natalie

stood there a moment and watched as he shut the door between them.

He was right again, of course. It would be easier with the hatred. But they'd have to put their hostility aside while they worked together.

And while they spent the night together under the same roof.

Without the hatred, the old temptations would be there. They couldn't give in to them.

Not ever.

That promise to David had sealed their fates and their futures.

Natalie went into her room and locked the door. It seemed an unnecessary and perhaps even small-minded gesture, but after everything that had happened, she wanted to take every security measure she could take.

The fatigue began to consume her as she dressed for bed, and she figured she would get some sleep whether her mind cooperated or not. However, she still needed to make that call to the caterer, and that had to come before bed.

She searched through the phone book, located a business number for Antoine Dupree. She dialed the number, but he obviously wasn't in. There wasn't even an answering machine or service. So, speaking with the man was yet something else that would have to wait until morning.

Surrendering to the fatigue, Natalie started toward

her bed. However, before her head could hit the pillow, the phone rang. She hurried across the room to answer it. It was Kitt.

"Glad you're finally home," Kitt said. "I've been worried about you."

"And I was worried about you." Natalie almost hated to bring up Dr. Benjamin, but it was necessary. After all, according to Macy, Kitt was part of Dr. Benjamin's project as well. After she told her, she asked, "You aren't pregnant or anything—"

"No. God, no. I took a pregnancy test, and I'm definitely without child. Maybe Dr. Benjamin decided that I wasn't one of the Cyrene Project's success stories. I told you that 4.0 grade-point average would come back to haunt you. You should have partied and cut classes like I did."

Natalie tried to smile. Failed. "How's Mom?"

Silence.

Natalie didn't have any adrenaline left in her body, but she forced herself to reach for her clothes so she could make the trip to her mother's house.

"Don't come back over here tonight," Kitt insisted, obviously knowing what Natalie was about to do. "You already have enough to deal with, and besides I have everything under control."

"Then why the silence?"

"Because you're not going to like what I have to tell you." Kitt paused. "After chatting with her, I'm getting ready to leave. I'm going to check her into the hospital where she'll have a full psychiatric evaluation in the morning."

Natalie sat down in the chaise near the phone. The hospitalization was necessary, but it didn't make it any easier to accept.

Sweet heaven.

Everything in her life had been turned upside down.

"I talked with a doctor—not Dr. Benjamin," Kitt quickly added. "And it's possible that Macy is experiencing some kind of psychotic break. It might be something simple—like all those herbs and tonics she's always taking. Or it might be something more serious. Anyway, she needs to be hospitalized so they can run some tests."

Natalie couldn't dispute any of that. Though she was furious with her mother for all the lies, she couldn't just turn her back on Macy. "Give me the name of the hospital, and I'll visit her in the morning."

More silence from Kitt. "Uh, that's probably not a very good idea."

Natalie tried to think of a reason her sister would say that, but other than the additional stress of such a visit on the baby, Natalie couldn't think of one. "Why not?"

"Because before I came downstairs to call you, Macy said some things."

"What things?"

Kitt mumbled something. Something that indicated she didn't want to be the messenger for this particular revelation. "Look, I'm not even sure where

Macy got her information or even if it's true. You know how mixed-up things are right now. Why don't we put this discussion on hold until I've had time to check things out?"

Natalie huffed. She didn't intend to beat around the bush. "Yes, I know things are mixed up, and I also know you're stalling. Tell me what Mom said. I'm a big girl, and I don't need to be protected."

"Okay, but brace yourself." Kitt added her own huff and a few more seconds of hesitation. "Macy said someone wants Rick and you dead."

Chapter Seven

A fish-out-of-water analogy came to mind as Rick looked around the guest room.

The place was really a guest suite with a sitting area and an adjoining bathroom. All three areas were decorated in varying shades of white and beige with lots of marble, granite and milky glass tiles to separate the rooms. It looked like something right out of a decorating magazine. A far cry from the modest house that he'd bought as a fixer-upper and hadn't yet quite gotten around to the fixing part.

For some reason, despite its too-perfect appearance, the suite felt like Natalie.

Not exactly a comforting thought.

But then, Rick hadn't thought for one minute that he could put Natalie out of his mind tonight. She was just up the hall, two doors down. In the very room where they'd apparently had sex. No. There wasn't a snowball's chance in Hades of his forgetting that.

Or her.

Still, he hadn't had a choice about staying at her house. After the SUV incident and Macy's bombshell about the Cyrene Project, Natalie was in no shape to be left alone.

He sank down onto the foot of the bed and took out his phone. He called his uncle Carlton, the only relative he had left alive. After what Macy had told them, it made Rick wonder if Carlton knew about the Cyrene Project. His uncle had certainly never mentioned it, and they'd had some long, soul-searching chats. Which meant Carlton had likely been kept in the dark. That made sense. His parents probably didn't want a lot of people to know they'd gotten involved in such a stupid experiment.

An experiment that had apparently severed a relationship between his mother and Carlton.

Strange.

If Dr. Benjamin hadn't come into their lives, Carlton might have ended up being his father. And that would have been fitting since Carlton was far more of a dad to him than his own father had been.

How had Carlton reacted to being dumped? Had he held it against Rick's parents? If so, he hadn't shown it.

Because Carlton and he were close, Rick had no plans to deliver the news of Natalie's pregnancy over the phone. But he did want to let his uncle know that he wouldn't be at the shop for the next few days. The timing couldn't have been worse, since he was already behind in work orders, but he'd just have to let his head mechanic take over for a while. Rick's first priority had to be Natalie and the baby.

"The baby," he repeated under his breath.

And he wondered how many times he would have to say it before it didn't sound so foreign. Maybe it would never feel natural, but he refused to believe that. Other men had faced fatherhood. Perhaps not under these exact circumstances. But they'd faced it since the beginning of time. He was a strong guy with a solid business and an equally solid foundation in life. This was not going to kick his butt.

He hoped.

But he did feel a lurch in his stomach when he thought about trying to hold a newborn in his calloused hands.

He was so in trouble here.

Carlton didn't answer either his home or cell phones so Rick left a message on his voice mail.

Rick checked the time. It was nearly 9:00 p.m. Hardly the ideal hour to be calling his doctor, but he was anxious to get the results of the lab tests, and he was equally anxious to keep his mind occupied so he'd stop thinking about all the things that were making him crazy.

He located Dr. Macomb's number in his phone book and worked his way to an employee at an answering service that he finally convinced to transfer his call to the doctor's home.

Rick was still waiting on hold when there was a small tap at the door.

"It's me," he heard Natalie say.

Oh, man.

This couldn't be good. He knew for a fact that Natalie was too exhausted and not inclined for a social visit. Plus, she would probably do just about anything to avoid seeing him tonight. She'd no doubt had her fill of him. So, that meant this was important.

"Come in," Rick invited.

She did. Natalie opened the door and peeked inside, probably to make sure he was dressed. Only when she was certain of that, did she step inside. She didn't come close. In fact, she stood mere inches away from the hall and a good twenty feet away from him.

Yet, it felt very close.

She wore a deep-purple gown and matching robe. Silk. The outfit skimmed along her entire body, stopping just above her bare ankles and feet. Not provocative, exactly.

Okay, it was provocative.

He could see the outline of nipples and the sweet curves of her hips. Not a waif's body. A woman's body.

And his male body reacted in a bad male sort of way. That reaction stopped, however, when he noticed the concern on her face.

"You're on the phone," she commented, and she turned as if to leave.

"I'm on hold, waiting for my doctor. I'm hoping the lab results are back." Rick paused. When Natalie didn't say anything, he gave her the prompt that she seemed to be waiting for. "What's wrong?"

She didn't answer right away. She adjusted the sash of her robe; it really didn't need an adjustment. it was tied snugly around her waist.

"Kitt just called," she explained. Natalie's forehead bunched up.

Yep. He was right. This was bad news, and Rick tried to prepare himself for it. However, he wasn't sure he was ready for anything else to go wrong.

"Kitt is taking my mother to the hospital because she seemed disoriented. They're going to do a physical and a psychiatric evaluation on her in the morning."

Okay. That wasn't quite as bad as he'd imagined. In fact, it was expected and even welcomed because he'd been worried about Macy and wanted her to get whatever help she needed. Still, it was obvious Natalie was having a little trouble dealing with it. No surprise there. This was her mother, and despite the vast differences in their personalities, and the lies that were just revealed, Natalie loved Macy.

"It's for the best," he tried to reassure her.

She nodded. "I know."

That calmly delivered *I know* caused him to get to his feet. "What else happened?"

Natalie opened her mouth. Closed it. Shook her head. "Macy told Kitt that someone wants to kill us."

"Hell."

Rick didn't know if the entire world was against them, or if it simply felt that way. If he hadn't been holding his phone, he would have thrown his hands in the air.

He wasn't sure which way to go with this, so he took the direct approach. "And did Macy have any details about this particular threat?"

"No. I'm not even sure she knows what she's saying. You saw what happened at her house."

Rick agreed. Macy obviously had problems thinking clearly. Still, he wasn't ready to dismiss anything just yet.

Obviously, neither was Natalie.

Rick almost went to her. To reassure her. To comfort her. After all, they'd already had a hugging session today, and one more probably wouldn't hurt.

But he stayed put.

Because he knew that *probably wouldn't hurt* was pure BS. In the long run, maybe even the short run, it would hurt.

"I just wanted you to know what Macy said," Natalie added. She made a vague motion in the direction of her room. She had already turned to walk away when Rick finally heard the doctor's voice on the other end of the line.

"Rick," Dr. Macomb said. "I was about to call you."

"With good news, I hope."

"Afraid not. I've already made some calls and have a colleague looking into the matter, but I don't think it's going to help."

Rick didn't even bother to groan or curse. He waited for the doctor to continue.

"Your blood samples and your lab results have simply disappeared."

WHILE Natalie waited on hold for her sister, she prayed for a change of luck. Heaven knew, Rick and she could use some sort of intervention, either divine, cosmic or otherwise. So far, nothing had gone their way. Fortunately though, that might all change after they spoke to Dr. Benjamin.

And they were within minutes of doing that.

Well, she hoped so.

Natalie had confirmed with a call that Dr. Benjamin was at his office. She thought that odd for a Sunday, but according to the doctor's answering service, he worked seven days a week. That was lucky for them because they knew where he was, and Rick was driving in that direction while he was on the phone with someone at the lab who was trying to locate his missing results.

She wanted to believe the missing lab tests were a coincidence. Ditto for the SUV. Ditto for her mother's thin grip on reality. But unfortunately, too many coincidences meant they probably weren't coincidences at all. And more, everything kept pointing to the culprit as Dr. Benjamin and his wretched Cyrene Project.

"Natalie," she finally heard her sister say. "The psychiatrist can't say for sure, but she thinks Mom might have some kind of chemical imbalance."

Natalie released the breath she'd been holding. "Good. That's a start." A chemical imbalance seemed a lot less serious than some of the alternatives—Alzheimer's or insanity. "Remember not to let Dr. Benjamin anywhere near her."

"Agreed. After what you told me about him, I don't want him on the same planet as us." Kitt cursed. "I can't believe he's that much of a psycho."

Psycho or obsessed. Or both. Either way, it had spelled trouble for them.

"How are you doing?" Kitt asked her.

Natalie understood that her sister's question encompassed more than just her well-being. It went much deeper than that. "It's going to take a while to come to grips with everything."

"Yeah. I know." Kitt paused. "And how's Rick handling this?"

As if he sensed that he was now part of their discussion, Rick glanced at her and lifted his left eyebrow.

"He's…good," Natalie said.

"Good?" Kitt repeated. "I doubt that. You two are probably at each other's throats by now."

"Not even close."

And that disturbed Natalie.

Already, she could feel herself being drawn back to him. Not just in a sexual way, either. Though that was there. But she was drawn to him in another way as well. In a way more intimate than sex.

Natalie would make sure that feeling didn't grow.

This was a nip-it-in-the-bud situation.

She'd made a promise to a dying man, and she intended to keep it.

She also intended to do whatever it took to regain control of her life. That started with answers.

"Kitt, I know you're busy with Mom, but I need you to do me a favor."

"Sure. What?"

"Could you try to contact Antoine Dupree? That's the caterer Mom hired for my party."

"Yeah. I remember the guy. He was prissy. And he wore red cowboy boots. He showed up that morning, barked out a few orders, fussed about some flower arrangements, and I didn't see him again."

Natalie tried to choose her words carefully so she wouldn't unnecessarily alarm her sister. "Did it seem as if he had a hidden agenda in being there?"

"What Natalie wants to know—did he drug us?" Rick clarified in a loud enough voice for Kitt to hear. He was obviously on hold with his own call, and since this had become a three-way conversation, Natalie clicked on the speakerphone function.

"I don't know about the drugging or the hidden

agenda, but I'll check on Dupree," Kitt volunteered. "I'll also ask about his staff. Come to think of it, I'm a little suspicious about the big bartender with the shaved head."

That grabbed Natalie's attention. "What about him?"

"Well, for one thing, he didn't know a lot about mixing drinks. That's a major liability for a person in his trade. I also noticed him talking on his cell phone a few times. I didn't think much about it that night, but it might mean something."

Yes. It might mean they were on the right track to finding the culprit. Of course, it could be the bartender was just a lousy employee who liked to make personal calls during business hours.

"Get me this guy's name, Kitt," Rick insisted.

"Give me an hour," Kitt said confidently.

Natalie knew it wasn't overconfidence. Her sister was a genius at that sort of thing. In fact, if Kitt hadn't been so tied up with Macy's health crisis, Natalie would have wanted her sister to sit in on this meeting with Dr. Benjamin.

Rick readjusted his phone. "Yes. I'm still here," he said to the person on the other end of the line while making the final turn into the parking lot.

"I have to go," Natalie explained to Kitt as Rick parked in front of Dr. Benjamin's office. "Call me if you learn anything about Mom's condition."

"Will do. And I'll call as soon as I have the bartender's name. Oh, and good luck with Dr. Benjamin. Slap him a few times for me, will you?"

Natalie had never considered herself a violent person, but heaven help her, she truly wouldn't mind slapping the doctor if he'd done what she thought he had. "Goodbye, Kitt."

Rick ended his call as well, shaking his head. "The lab results are gone," he let her know. "There's no record of my blood samples ever being logged in and no record of them ever being run."

"And what is the lab planning to do about that?" she wanted to know.

"My doctor still has the receipt of delivery for the blood vials so he knows the lab received them."

Natalie considered that a moment. "So, someone is covering up for the person who drugged you?"

"Looks that way. That's why my doctor intends to turn the matter over to the police."

Of course he did. And that meant everything would come out in the open.

Everything.

Her pregnancy. Her mother's bizarre behavior. Dr. Benjamin's involvement. Rick and she really needed to get answers about the Cyrene Project that they could pass on to the police.

"You can skip this visit with Dr. Benjamin, you know," Rick reminded her again.

"So you've said."

She slammed the car door but stopped when she realized Rick wasn't following her.

Natalie turned and saw him retrieve his jacket from the back seat. The jacket they'd picked up at his house only minutes earlier. Because she'd been so preoccupied with everything else, she hadn't realized just how odd that was. It was summer in San Antonio. The temperature would soar into the high nineties. Hardly jacket weather.

"What are you doing?" she asked.

But an answer wasn't necessary. Rick stayed in the car, concealed behind the tinted windows. She watched as Rick took a leather shoulder holster and gun from the jacket. That didn't do a lot to steady her heart. The unsteadiness went up a notch when he strapped on the holster, slipped in the gun and then put on his jacket to conceal both. He got out of the car.

Once she regained her breath, she fell in step alongside him. "You think the gun is necessary?"

"Could be. We don't know how Dr. Benjamin will react when we confront him. That's why I didn't want you to come. And don't bother reminding me that he wouldn't hurt the baby because we might not be dealing with a man who's totally sane."

Natalie swallowed hard. She didn't want to believe her life was in danger, but Rick was right. Still, they needed answers, and that meant this was a chance they had to take.

He stopped just outside the office door and stared

down at her. But he did more than stare. He stepped closer and leaned his mouth in close to her ear. "Look, I know you'll do this no matter how much I object, but make just one concession for me. If things turn ugly, swear to me that you'll get out of the way."

With that, he pulled back so they could make eye contact. She opened her mouth to remind him that he could be in danger as well, but Rick merely aimed a firm glance at her stomach.

Oh, mercy.

Natalie knew what that glance meant. He was reminding her that if she were in danger, then so was the baby. And he was right about that as well.

"I won't take any unnecessary chances," she promised him. She started to leave it at that, but her mouth and her brain just didn't cooperate. "And neither will you."

He blinked. Then, he groaned. "What the hell is happening to us?"

She didn't think he meant the pregnancy and the rest of the craziness. This was about that blasted empathy they were feeling for each other.

"I can blame my reaction on hormones," she said, trying not to sound too smug.

He waited a moment, staring at her. He was so close that she could see the emotion in his eyes. She could see his mouth tighten as well, as if he were fighting a smile. Or maybe he was fighting the urge to use some profanity. She definitely understood his confusion.

"I have this need to protect you," he informed her. He said it as if it were a death sentence.

"Well, I could go all bravado and tell you that I don't need your protection, but I'm not an idiot."

His mouth tightened even more. "You need me," Rick mumbled.

Natalie wasn't sure if it was a question or not, but she nodded. "And if you think that was an easy admission for me to make—"

"I know it wasn't."

He shifted slightly, turning away from her. It didn't help. It darn sure didn't put much distance between them. He was still so close that she could smell the remnants of the laundry detergent in his black T-shirt and jeans.

That outfit, paired with his usual snakeskin boots, was Rick's usual attire. He was definitely a jeans kind of person. Rugged. Independent. A Harley-riding cowboy. And, as he'd pointed out, he could kick some serious butt if necessary. For this moment in time in her life, he was as close to ideal as she would get.

"Let's declare a truce," she suggested.

"From what?"

And he was serious, too.

Unfortunately, Natalie realized this conversation had gone in the exact direction she didn't want it to go. "I'll keep my hormones in check. You'll do the same."

His mouth didn't tighten now. It bent into a half smile. A sarcastic one. "Yeah. Right."

He didn't elaborate. Thank goodness. Rick simply nodded, continued to stare at her, and after he paused for several long seconds, he opened the door. "We'd better go inside before I say something we'd both regret."

Natalie totally agreed.

The cool air from inside the office building washed over her and cleared her head of their troubling conversation. Not that she needed such measures for head-clearing. She suddenly felt focused, and she knew this could be the beginning of an explanation that would help her start to understand what had happened.

Well, maybe.

And she might just have to accept that no explanation would help. There might be nothing anyone could say that would make her come to terms with what had happened.

Rick and she didn't stop at the receptionist's desk, though the woman sprang up from her chair and asked if she could help them. However, the alarm on her face wasn't as polite as her question. The woman's politeness faded when they continued past her and headed straight for the doctor's office.

Dr. Benjamin was there—wearing a white lab coat and seated behind his pristine desk. And, they noted thankfully, he was alone. It saved them from ousting a patient or a colleague so he would see them immediately.

Rick and Natalie went in and faced him.

The doctor didn't seem the least bit alarmed by the intrusion. He calmly removed his reading glasses and set them aside. He also took a leisurely sip of tea.

"This is obviously about the pregnancy," Dr. Benjamin concluded.

She didn't know whether to be surprised or relieved. "You bet it is," Natalie confirmed.

The phone buzzed, and the doctor answered it. Natalie listened while he assured someone, probably his receptionist, that he was indeed okay and that he was not to be disturbed.

And that disturbed Natalie.

He certainly wasn't acting like a man who was guilty of a crime. He was reacting as if Rick and she were there under totally normal circumstances.

"We know all about the Cyrene Project," Rick started. Natalie sat down, but not Rick. He leaned over the desk, violating the doctor's personal space and glaring at him. "And we figure you drugged us so you could continue with your little experiment."

The doctor flexed his thick, graying eyebrows. "Oh, I definitely wanted the project to continue. And it pleases me that there'll finally be a phase-two baby. But you have it wrong—I didn't drug you."

"I don't believe you," Rick concluded.

Natalie echoed the same.

"I don't know how to convince you otherwise. I'm a doctor, and I run a reputable practice—"

"You were trying to play God," Rick interrupted.

"It might appear that way on the surface, but there's more to it." The doctor took another sip of tea. "Intelligent, healthy citizens will make a better civilization."

"Didn't Hitler say that?" Rick fired back.

Dr. Benjamin sat up in his chair. "I assure you, I had nothing sinister in mind. I merely paired couples who were more likely to produce intelligent, superior babies. That's why I thought the two of you would make a perfect match."

Natalie groaned. Well, that confirmed what her mother had said, and explained why Macy and her family doctor had practically pushed her into Rick's arms.

"You're both superior, you know," the doctor continued. His tone made it seem as if that excused everything he'd done, and in his mind it probably did.

"So we've been told." Rick's tone, however, accepted no such excuse. "But don't expect either of us to thank you for that genetic interference. And by the way, you still haven't convinced me that you're innocent of drugging us. You're the only one with a motive."

"But I'm not. What if I were to provide the names of the people whom I think might be guilty?"

"Names would be a good start," Natalie assured him, and she moved to the edge of her seat.

"Well, for one, you'll want to talk with Dr. Isabella Henderson."

Natalie should have already considered that. The name was as familiar to her as Dr. Benjamin's; Natalie had known the woman her entire life.

"Dr. Isabella Henderson—your business partner?" Rick questioned.

The doctor nodded. "My *former* partner."

"Former? Since when?" Natalie wanted to know. "Dr. Henderson was working here just a few days ago when you ran the pregnancy test on me."

"That's right. I believe that's the day Isabella and I parted company."

"Seems a little sudden, and I don't care much for the timing. Would you mind explaining why she left?" Rick insisted.

"I don't mind, but I'm not sure you'll understand. I certainly don't."

Impatient, Natalie pressed harder. "Give it a try. We're listening."

"All right. Isabella helped me start the Cyrene Project thirty-one years ago when we were completing our residencies. But a person can change a lot in thirty-one years. Trust me—Isabella changed, and that change was dramatic, especially in the past few weeks. She says now that she wants to be respected in the medical community, and she's afraid she'll be ruined professionally and lose funding for her latest research if the powers-that-be learn about the Cyrene Project."

This just kept getting deeper and deeper, but

Natalie hoped that the deepness didn't extend to her siblings. "Are Rick and I the only people involved with phase two?" Natalie wanted to know.

"All the phase-one babies were paired, but if you're asking if your sister was drugged, I doubt it. Unlike you, she doesn't have gaps in her memory, and there's no indication that she's pregnant."

That was true, but it didn't make Natalie feel any better. They needed to get to the bottom of this so she could make sure her sister was safe.

Her brother, Wyatt, was also a concern, but she knew for a fact that Wyatt could take care of himself. A drugging doctor with an insane plan probably wouldn't pose much of a threat to a Justice Department operative like Wyatt. In fact, if Wyatt weren't in the Middle East on assignment, Natalie would have contacted him to see if he could help.

"Where's Dr. Henderson?" Rick demanded.

Dr. Benjamin used his notepad to write down an address. He passed it to Natalie, and she slipped it in her purse. "That's her new business office. Isabella will deny involvement, of course, and she might have a valid reason for that."

"And why is that?" Rick snarled.

"She could be innocent. I have no proof that will condemn or exonerate her."

Rick and Natalie exchanged glances. Frustrated ones. "That's right," Natalie commented. "You said you had some *names* for us. So, who's next on your list?" She waited for him to bring up someone on the catering staff.

"There's only one other person who I believe could be responsible for this." Dr. Benjamin rubbed his eyes, and a disconcerting sound rumbled deep in his throat. "Macy's personal assistant, Troy."

Neither Rick nor Natalie said anything, but he slowly sank down in the chair beside her. "Explain that please," Natalie insisted.

"Of course. Troy is yet another offspring of the Cyrene Project. And before you accuse me of some kind of conspiracy, I didn't know who he was. Not until two days ago. I'd lost contact with Troy's mother and had no idea where he was. I certainly had no idea he was working for Macy."

"Keep going." Rick made a circular motion with his hand when the doctor paused.

"I got suspicious of Troy when Macy started having headaches and problems with her memory. I decided to have him investigated in case he was doing something to harm her. That's when I learned who he really is."

Natalie only wished she'd noticed her mother's problems sooner and had had Troy investigated herself. There was something totally unnerving about the man's connection to the Cyrene Project and now his involvement with Macy. Natalie made a mental note to fire Troy and get a restraining order to keep him away from anyone in her family—especially her mother—and from Rick.

"Did you happen to ask Troy why he's working for my mother?" she asked.

"I did. He claims he wanted to learn more about the Cyrene Project and that his parents refused to discuss it with him. He said when he went to Macy that she felt sorry for him and offered him a job. That was about two months ago."

Natalie did a quick memory search—had her mother's problems started about that time? She didn't know, but she intended to find out. And by God, Troy had better not be in her path if he was responsible for her mother's rapid decline in health. If he was, Natalie was going after him. Judging from Rick's fierce expression, however, she'd have to wait in line.

"I'll deal with Troy," Rick muttered and then stared at the doctor. "And you think Troy could have had something to do with drugging us?"

"Absolutely. That's why I told Macy to get rid of him. She wouldn't listen to reason. She wouldn't believe that Troy is a threat."

That one word stopped Natalie cold. "What kind of *threat?*"

"To you, of course," the doctor said without hesitation.

That brought Natalie to her feet. "What do you mean?"

He shrugged. "I mean that Troy and I have discussed this as recently as yesterday. He's a very troubled man, and he blames all of his problems on the Cyrene Project. He'd like to erase its existence. And I can say with certainty that he believes both of you would be better off dead."

Chapter Eight

Rick tried to process everything he'd just heard. He could understand Dr. Benjamin implicating his former partner, Isabella Henderson. However, it was more than a surprise to hear that Troy might have had some part in this.

Or had he?

Even if Troy was opposed to the Cyrene Project, would the man really have tried to kill them?

Several days ago, Rick would have never believed it, but he didn't know what to believe now.

Man, there was a lot coming at Natalie and him. After hearing what Dr. Benjamin had to say, they obviously needed to question Troy and Dr. Isabella Henderson. They also had missing lab results to deal with. Oh, and they had to come to terms with the fact they were going to be parents in about eight months. Rick considered himself a hands-on, do-it-yourself kind of person, but it was obvious this wasn't something that Natalie or he could or should do alone.

This needed to be turned over to the police.

Rick looked at Natalie. "Dr. Benjamin could be lying to save his own butt," he reminded her.

She nodded, but there was no certainty in it. Natalie was shaken. For good reason, too. Her mother's personal assistant was likely a wacko. Or worse—a potential killer.

Troy might not have been the driver in that SUV, but if he were deranged, he could have hired someone to play dangerous games.

Of course, that wasn't Rick's primary theory. He'd meant that part about Dr. Benjamin lying, and the doctor was still his number-one suspect.

Rick stood and took Natalie's hand so that she would do the same. She did. And she even leaned against him, though Rick wasn't sure she realized what she was doing.

He was ready to deliver some parting words to the doctor when he heard his phone beep. He glanced down at the screen and saw the text page from his uncle Carlton. The message was simple.

Meet me at your shop. It's important.

Great. His uncle rarely paged him. However, it was entirely possible that Macy or even Natalie's sister had called Carlton to let him know what was going on. That would lead to a conversation that Rick didn't have time for.

"Who paged you?" Natalie whispered, obviously noting his new concern.

"Uncle Carlton. I need to meet him at the shop."

And he would meet him. That *important* part meant it wasn't something Rick could avoid. However, it would have to be a quick detour because Rick really wanted to have a few words with Dr. Henderson and Troy.

So that he'd get Dr. Benjamin's attention, Rick aimed his index finger at the man. "Since you engineered my DNA, so to speak, you know what I'm capable of doing. And you know I'll figure out if you're behind this. If you are behind it, I'll make sure you regret it."

The doctor calmly leaned back in his chair. "I'm not intimidated by your threats."

Rick glared at him. "Well, if you're smart, you should be." He continued the glare until the doctor looked away.

Certain that he'd gotten his point across, Rick took Natalie out of there. Just having her and his baby in the same room as that monster made his stomach turn.

Rick didn't waste any time in what he had to say. "We should go to police headquarters and tell them everything we've learned," Rick told Natalie the moment they were out of Dr. Benjamin's office.

She stopped and looked up at him. "If we do, they'll want to talk to my mother. She's not up to that right now."

"Yeah." Rick didn't have to add more because he could feel his own hesitancy and knew Natalie was feeling the same. "We can wait until the psychiatric evaluation is finished. But in the meantime, we get Troy out of her house and make sure he doesn't come back."

Natalie nodded. "I hope we can keep Macy in the hospital until we can figure out what to do."

Yes, that was the problem—figuring out what to do and hoping they'd make the right decision. Too much was at stake to fail.

"I'll talk with Dr. Henderson," Rick let Natalie know.

She looked at him. "And she'll likely stonewall us. Especially if she's guilty."

"Possibly. But she might have some clues that will help us nail Dr. Benjamin."

They got in Natalie's car, and Rick began to drive toward the shop. The car was hot from sitting outside in the blazing sun. He could smell the leather seats and his own sweat. But it wasn't that particular scent that filled the car. It was Natalie. She was wearing some kind of light musky perfume. Or maybe that was just her natural scent. Either way, Rick decided to do away with it. He lowered the window for a few seconds to let the outside air rush through the car.

It didn't help.

Her scent was still there.

And his body was well aware of that.

He tried to take her advice and declare a hormonal truce. His body laughed at him. Heck, Rick laughed at himself. The only way to get out of this intact was to hurry up and find the truth. Only then would he be able to distance himself from Natalie. In the meantime, he made a vow to occupy his mind with learning the truth and preparing Natalie for what they were perhaps about to face.

"Macy might have told Carlton that you're pregnant," Rick commented. And he waited for that to sink in.

It didn't take long.

Natalie groaned. "He'll be upset."

That was truly sugar-coating it. Carlton wouldn't just be upset. He'd be downright furious.

Unlike Macy, Carlton had never tried to push the two of them together. Just the opposite. In fact, Carlton had shown outright disdain for Natalie after David's death. His uncle had certainly made it clear that they should abide by the deathbed promise they'd made to David and never have anything else to do with each other.

Sometimes Rick wondered why his uncle was so adamant about keeping that promise. The only thing he'd been able to come up with was that Carlton and David had been very close. Perhaps even closer than either man had been to Rick. Maybe Carlton felt that closeness meant he had to look after David's best interests—forever.

"If you're not up to dealing with Carlton, I can drop you off at home first," Rick offered. And he could also arrange for someone to stay with her. He definitely didn't want her alone until everything had been resolved.

"No. Avoiding Carlton won't change the truth. I'm pregnant. Your uncle will have to learn to deal with it."

She adjusted her slim rose-colored skirt, trying to slide it so that it covered more of her legs. He could hear the silk fabric whisper against her skin. That sound, coupled with her scent, was yet another reminder of Natalie that he didn't need. Best to think of her as a fellow victim rather than the desirable woman that she was.

Now, if only his body would agree with what his brain had decided.

"How *do* we deal with this pregnancy, Rick?" Her voice was feathery-light. And frustrated.

He got his mind off her skirt and perfume and concentrated on her question. "It's a cliché, but we do it one day at a time. We find out who's responsible, and we make them pay."

She waited a moment. "And then what?"

Rick didn't think that question was about drugging culprits or the confrontation they were about to have with his uncle. "I've always liked kids," he said, hoping it was the right thing to say. This was definitely touchy territory. Natalie was just coming to terms with the baby, and he didn't want to force himself into her life.

Still, he was there. In her life.

"Liking kids and wanting them are two totally different things," she fired back.

Ah. So, that's where this was leading. He got it now.

"I won't walk away from this baby," he assured her. Though he was in that touchy territory again, mainly because it'd be easier for Natalie if he *did* just walk away.

But he couldn't.

He *wouldn't*.

Rick didn't need a long, soul-searching session to figure that out. This baby was his, and he was going to take responsibility for the child—even if Natalie had no intentions of letting him do that.

As if sensing the battle going on inside him, she turned and stared at him. There was the sound of silk again, and for just a moment he met her gaze.

"We can share custody or something," he suggested.

"Or something?" she questioned.

Rick didn't have a clue what that *or something* was, but he was open to any and all suggestions that would allow him to be a part of his child's life.

"First, we'll catch the slime who did this to us," he explained. "Then, we'll concentrate on whatever plans we need to make for the baby." Rick slid his hand over hers. "You're not alone in this, Natalie. I'm right here with you."

"Yes." But she made it sound as if that weren't a good thing.

Rick understood. This camaraderie and closeness was making him feel, well, close. To Natalie. And there was nothing he could do to stop it.

She glanced down at his hand. She didn't say anything. Nor did she move away. Rick did though. He didn't know why he had this burning need to comfort her, but he did. Despite that need, he did the right thing. He moved his hand and reminded himself that she was not his for the taking. Just because she carried his child, that didn't mean it entitled him to anything.

With that depressing but totally accurate thought, Rick pulled into the parking lot of his shop and stopped the car.

"This place is so you," she mumbled, looking up at the sign perched over the front door.

Rick tried to figure out what she meant by that, and he tried to see the shop through her eyes. To Natalie, it probably didn't look like much. Sixteen hundred square feet of wood, limestone and glass. Not a classy place but a place where real bikers would feel at home.

The sign that she was staring at wasn't classy, either, but Rick did consider it a classic. It was a 1940s scarlet neon sign that simply said Rick's Place. He'd found it six years earlier at an architectural salvage store and had bought it on the spot. That sign had become the inspiration and the cornerstone for his business.

"Did you just insult me?" Rick had to ask.

Her eyes widened. "No. Of course not."

"Well, you did say the place was so me."

"It is. But I meant that in a good way. It's functional, but you've added some interesting elements that reflect your personality. Like the rustic pine door and the vintage sign. Nostalgic but manly."

"Thanks." He thought about that a moment. Frowned. "I think."

She chuckled, reached over and rubbed the frown line that had formed on his forehead. "Don't look for hidden meanings. It was a compliment. You found your niche in the world, and that's a good thing."

"You found yours," he pointed out.

"Yes." And she paused, stared at the sign. "But I was getting to the point in my life where I was asking—is this all there is? Get up, go to work, business trips, phone calls. The same thing day in and day out. Routine punctuated with just enough excitement to keep me from tossing it all in."

Rick could certainly relate. "Well, there's nothing routine about what we're facing now."

"No, and that's why this is so weird. I mean, when I first learned I was pregnant, I panicked. I thought this has to be the worst that's ever happened. I panicked again at the thought of just holding a baby.

But now…" She stopped, drew back her hand and shook her head. "Sorry. Apparently pregnancy hormones also make me babble like an idiot."

"It didn't sound idiotic to me. You're just adjusting. That's what people do, Natalie. They get hit with something they think they can never handle, and they handle it because they don't have a choice."

She frowned. "That sounds suspiciously like a pep talk."

"Guilty." Because he had that moronic need to touch her again, he gripped the steering wheel instead.

"I've missed talking to you," she said. "And don't look at me. Don't even say anything. Because I shouldn't be saying this. But you were my friend, and I lost you the day David died."

Rick had to look at her. Yep, and he had to touch her, too. He caught onto her chin and turned it in his direction. That's when he spotted that tear in her eye. She was blinking frantically to keep it from falling. She failed. It fell anyway, and Rick leaned over and kissed it away.

He didn't linger with that cheek kiss, and he didn't stay close because he knew they were sitting on a keg of emotional dynamite. If he kissed her now, really kissed her the way he wanted to, it would violate his own personal rules. He wouldn't take advantage of her vulnerability.

"Don't remember anything I just said," she mumbled. "Swear it."

"Consider it sworn. I won't remember anything. The drunken-babe rule applies here."

She stared at him. "Excuse me?"

"It's a rule that decent guys follow. I'll just pretend you're a drunk attractive woman whom I've met in a bar. Anything said under the influence of alcohol— or in your case, pregnancy hormones—will not be added to my long-term memory." He snapped his fingers. "It'll be gone in five seconds. Promise. Because I'm a decent guy."

She smiled, but it faded and became a heavy sigh. "We should go in and face Carlton."

Rick nodded. It was a good suggestion and a lot safer than what they'd just experienced.

"Is Carlton even here?" she asked, obviously determined to change the subject.

Rick pointed to a black Mustang. "That's his car, but I don't see him. He has a key so he's probably inside. Waiting. And in case you missed it—that's your cue to go home so you won't have to put yourself through this."

Any remnant of tears and vulnerability faded. "You're not going to face him alone. I'm doing this with you," Natalie insisted, getting out of the car.

Rick did the same, after making sure she noticed that he gave her an eye roll, and they made their way to the side entrance that led directly to his office. He stopped though when Natalie's cell phone rang.

"It's Kitt," Natalie said, glancing down at the name on the screen.

Rick listened as Natalie filled her sister in on what they'd learned from Dr. Benjamin. That explanation was followed by a short silence, and then Natalie ended the call and looked at him.

"The bartender's name is Brandon Stevens," Natalie relayed to him. "The caterer says he doesn't know anything about him. He hired the guy on the spot when the regular bartender didn't show up to do the party."

So, that made the man a suspect. It didn't, however, make him guilty of anything.

"Kitt's going to keep digging," Natalie added.

Rick knew she would, and he welcomed the help. While Kitt was on the path of Brandon Stevens, Natalie and he could concentrate on the two doctors involved.

And the inevitable confrontation with his uncle.

He tested the door. It was unlocked. Rick instinctively latched onto Natalie's arm and moved her behind him before he opened the door. He also slipped his hand into his jacket just in case it wasn't Carlton inside.

And just in case he needed to reach for his gun.

Natalie didn't huff or sigh. The incident with the SUV had no doubt changed all of that. From now on, they had to err on the side of caution.

"Carlton?" Rick called out.

He eased open the door and was greeted by the cool air of a working air conditioner. Rick made a mental note to thank his employees for taking care of that for him. He walked through his office, keeping Natalie safely behind him.

"I'm over here," Carlton answered.

Without leaving his office doorway, Rick glanced around the work bay and spotted Carlton. He was examining a custom Harley that was in the final stages of being rebuilt.

"You do good work," Carlton commented, tipping his head toward the Harley.

Small talk. Rick knew it wouldn't do much to reduce his stress levels. He stepped inside the work bay, and Natalie joined him.

Carlton straightened back up and spared Natalie a glance before fastening his attention on Rick. "Macy called and told me what happened."

His uncle's comment sounded grim and ominous, but it didn't really explain anything.

"You saw my mother?" Natalie asked.

Carlton shook his head. "No. She borrowed a cell phone from a nurse and called me from the hospital."

Rick ignored his uncle's obvious disapproval of Natalie and took the direct approach so he could quickly end this conversation. "And what exactly did Macy tell you?"

Carlton stuffed his hands into the pockets of his perfectly tailored khakis. The gesture was relaxed enough, but there was nothing relaxed about Carlton's expression.

Rick stared into the man's eyes, so genetically similar to his own, and waited for him to finish. The resemblance didn't stop there. People often mistook Carlton for Rick's older brother. They were the same height, same build, same coloring.

"Macy said that Natalie is pregnant with your baby," Carlton finally responded.

That was apparently it, the extent of Macy's explanation—which was obviously only the beginning of the story. Rick was about to gear up to add more info, but his uncle spoke before Rick could.

"How the hell could you do this?" Carlton snapped, and that snap was directed at Natalie.

It might as well have been aimed at Rick because it riled him to the core.

"Hey, wait a minute," Rick said at the exact moment that Natalie said, "This wasn't our fault."

But Carlton ignored both of them and continued with his voice raised. "Have you two forgotten about the promise you made to David?"

"No." Rick walked closer to his uncle. "But before you make any more accusations, hear us out. Someone drugged us. We had sex. Now, Natalie's pregnant."

That immediately reduced the anger in Carlton's expression and voice. "You're serious?"

"Oh, yeah."

Carlton hesitated a moment, volleying glances between Natalie and Rick. Finally, he cursed. "This has to do with the damn Cyrene Project, doesn't it?"

Natalie groaned. "You obviously know about that."

"I do. And I didn't approve of it when your parents agreed to participate, and I don't approve now."

"Welcome to the club," Rick mumbled, but he couldn't help but wonder if Carlton's disapproval was because of the project itself or because his mother's involvement in the project was what had caused her to sever her relationship with Carlton.

"Is Dr. Benjamin responsible for this, too?" Carlton demanded.

"Maybe. Or maybe it's the other doctor who started this idiotic project. Dr. Isabella Henderson. Then, there's Troy, Macy's assistant. According to Dr. Benjamin, Troy might be a wacko nut job who wants to hurt us because he's opposed to the Cyrene Project."

Carlton scrubbed his hand over his face. "It could be any or all of them. You're not dealing with rational people, Rick. You're dealing with people who think they have a right to play God."

"Yeah. I figured that out." Because it no longer seemed necessary, Rick eased his hand away from his gun. "It doesn't change what happened to Natalie and me."

"No." Carlton shook his head. It was a gesture of both sympathy and disgust. "So, what will you do about this baby?"

"Give birth to it," Natalie supplied.

"Love it. Raise it," Rick added.

Carlton's jaw muscles stirred against each other.

"The baby never should have been conceived. It's part of the very project that's ruined lives."

Anger spiked through Rick, and he didn't even try to keep his temper in check. "I won't let you talk about my child that way."

"It's the truth."

Rick had to fight hard to keep from slugging his own uncle. He pointed to the door. "It would be a really good time for you to leave."

Carlton looked as if Rick had struck him. "You can't mean that."

"Oh, but I do." In fact, Rick had never been more certain of anything.

Carlton cursed again and shot Natalie one more nasty glare before he stormed toward the door and slammed it behind him.

"Well, that was pleasant," Rick grumbled. Why had he come here with Natalie? Oh, yeah. Because he was an idiot. He should have insisted that she go home because he knew in his heart what his uncle's reaction would be. "I'm sorry you had to witness that."

"You don't have to apologize for anything Carlton says. Besides, he's just shocked."

"Still, that gives him no reason to talk about our baby that way."

Natalie touched his arm. Rubbed gently. It was obviously an attempt to calm him. It didn't work.

"It must be hard for Carlton," Natalie continued. "He hates me because of what happened to David."

"He has no right to hate you. I was there that night when David walked in on us. I kissed you— *voluntarily*. And I'm tired of Carlton aiming the blame at you."

"We're on the same side again," Natalie pointed out, frowning.

Yes. And it might stay that way for a while.

She paced a moment and stopped in front of him. "How do we get past what happened with David?" she asked. "How do we ever come to terms with it?"

"I don't know. You'd think with what we went through that there'd be nothing left between us."

"You'd think," Natalie agreed.

Rick was about to do something stupid—like elaborate on that, but he decided there was nothing he could say that would make things better. They weren't going to come to terms with this.

"It's a shame we can't just apply Carlton's philosophy and hate each other."

He looked at her at the exact moment she looked at him. The air between them changed. Or something. Rick didn't want to explore that something. In fact, he knew he should just step away. After all, Natalie and he were alone, and along with that air-changing thing, the expression on her face—her beautiful face—was causing him to think things he should never think.

Uh-huh. No way.

But he thought them.

It surprised him when he felt himself move. Natalie moved. Closer to him. Her eyelids fluttered down, and it took him a moment to realize why. He was moving in on her. He was lowering his head and closing the already narrow gap of space between them.

"I'll regret this," he heard himself mumble a moment before his mouth touched hers.

The jolt was instant. Intense. The air didn't just change. It began to sizzle.

Everything began to sizzle.

She tasted like everything he'd ever been denied but desperately wanted. She tasted like sin. Like hope. Like redemption.

Like Natalie.

She didn't back away after that initial taste. Nope. She slid her arms around his neck. First one. Then, the other. And she inched closer.

Rick did some inching of his own. He hooked his arm around her waist and hauled her to him. And he quit arguing with himself. Quit thinking. Instead, he took everything she was offering.

Everything.

Their bodies came together. It was a perfect fit. Just as he'd known it would be. Her breasts against his chest. Touching everywhere.

He deepened the kiss with his tongue. Still no resistance from Natalie. In fact, she made a throaty moan of pleasure and approval.

And that's when Rick knew he was in a helluva lot of trouble.

Still, he continued the kiss. Continued to deepen it. Their bodies adjusted, fighting to get closer as the heat between them rose.

"This is so wrong," Natalie mumbled against his mouth.

But she didn't stop.

She went back for a second round, and since Rick was past the point of logic, he made sure that second round was worth it. Finally, Natalie pulled away. A good thing, too. He was within seconds of dragging her to the floor. Hardly appropriate behavior. He was about to tell her that, too.

But he heard the slight sound.

It took him a moment to realize the sound hadn't come from Natalie. It took him yet another moment to realize it hadn't come from him.

"What happened?" Natalie asked, blinking and obviously trying to focus. She eased her arms from around his neck and stepped back.

Rick stepped back as well, lifted his head and caught a whiff of smoke.

He spun around, trying to detect the source, and it didn't take him long before he spotted the flames. They were bright and hot, eating their way through the back wall.

His shop was on fire.

Chapter Nine

"Fire!" Rick shouted.

Natalie whirled around and followed his startled gaze to see orange flames snaking along the wall adjacent to Rick's office. And there was smoke. Thin, black wisps, but the wisps were quickly growing into smothering clouds.

Her heart kicked into overdrive.

Obviously, so did Rick's. He raced across the shop area and grabbed a fire extinguisher that'd been mounted on the wall. Natalie followed his lead, looking around until she located another extinguisher on the other side of the open bay area. She hurried to retrieve it as Rick began to spray the flames.

Natalie sprayed the foam as well, but it didn't take her long to realize that this was a losing battle. The fire was spreading. Fast. And she could feel the brutal heat scorching her face.

Rick obviously realized the same thing because he

dropped the extinguisher, caught onto her arm and began running toward the door. In just those few steps, the smoke began to close in around them. It was dark and thick. Suffocating.

Natalie tossed her fire extinguisher aside, cupped her hand over her nose and mouth to try and stop herself from taking too much of it in.

She thought of the baby. Of the danger. The slam of adrenaline and the smoke couldn't be good for their unborn child, but there was nothing she could do about it except get out of there as fast as possible.

Rick fought through the smoke while keeping a firm grip on her. They made it to the front of the shop to the rustic pine door flanked on both sides by windows covered with metal security shutters. Natalie couldn't see outside, but she hoped that someone nearby had already called the fire department.

Rick reached for the brass doorknob and immediately jerked back his hand.

"It's scalding hot," he informed her.

Oh, mercy.

Natalie filled in the blanks. If the doorknob was hot, then the fire had likely spread to the front of the building. Or maybe that was the point of origin. If they tried to get out that way, they'd no doubt be engulfed in flames.

That robbed her of what little breath she had left.

She refused to give in to the panic. She had to concentrate on getting out of there and staying alive because if something happened to her, it also happened to the baby.

Rick tightened his grip on her arm and, with her in tow, he raced across the work bay, dodging parts and motorcycles.

"Please tell me there's another exit," Natalie shouted.

"There is, on the other side of the building."

The smoke was so thick that she didn't even know they'd reached another door until Rick stopped. He shoved her inside. It was a bathroom and not as smoky as the rest of the building. She automatically reached for the light switch, only to realize the power wasn't on. Thankfully, she realized that, of course, Rick knew where he was going.

They made their way to a pair of pedestal sinks. Rick let go of her so he could open the mottled-glass window high above them. Natalie felt the fresh air and automatically moved toward it. She had to get out of there for the sake of the baby. Every moment she spent in the smoke was a moment she could be endangering their child.

Rick scooped her into his arms and lifted her toward that window. It was a narrow opening, but because she knew she had no choice, Natalie squeezed her way through it. Rick kept a firm grip on her arm until her feet were on the ground outside.

"Run!" he shouted.

Her instincts were certainly screaming for her to

do just that. But her instincts were also telling her to make sure Rick was safe. After all, he'd saved her life. She couldn't just run away and not help him.

He could die.

The thought flashed though her head, but Natalie forced it aside and stuck her hand back through the window. Rick was already moving in her direction, but she caught onto his jeans anyway and pulled hard. It didn't take much, and he came out of the window, landing on his feet.

"Run!" he yelled, sounding relieved and annoyed. The annoyed part was probably because she hadn't obeyed his order the first time.

With his hand clutching hers, they raced down the sidewalk, away from the building and toward a crowd that had by now started to gather.

Natalie glanced back to see that the flames were already on the roof, and they were tearing through the building. There wouldn't be much to save unless the fire department got there in a hurry.

Rick grabbed his cell phone from his pocket and pressed in 911. "I need to report a fire."

And he gave them the address. Not frantically but calmly. Natalie didn't have a clue how he could be so calm after what they'd just experienced.

"If one unit is already on the way, I need an ambulance," Rick added, surprising her. "There was a pregnant woman trapped inside. She's out now, but she needs to see a doctor immediately."

OFFICIAL OPINION POLL

ANSWER 3 QUESTIONS AND WE'LL SEND YOU
4 FREE BOOKS AND A FREE GIFT!

0074823 | FREE GIFT CLAIM # 3953

YOUR OPINION COUNTS!

Please tick TRUE or FALSE below to express your opinion about the following statements:

Q1 Do you believe in "true love"?

"TRUE LOVE HAPPENS ONLY ONCE IN A LIFETIME."
○ TRUE
○ FALSE

Q2 Do you think marriage has any value in today's world?

"YOU CAN BE TOTALLY COMMITTED TO SOMEONE WITHOUT BEING MARRIED."
○ TRUE
○ FALSE

Q3 What kind of books do you enjoy?

"A GREAT NOVEL MUST HAVE A HAPPY ENDING."
○ TRUE
○ FALSE

YES, I have scratched the area below.

Please send me the **4 FREE BOOKS** and **FREE GIFT** for which I qualify. I understand I am under no obligation to purchase any books, as explained on the back of this card.

I7II

Mrs/Miss/Ms/Mr   Initials

BLOCK CAPITALS PLEASE

Surname

Address

Postcode

THE READER SERVICE™
FREE BOOK OFFER
FREEPOST CN81
CROYDON
CR9 3WZ

NO STAMP
NECESSARY
IF POSTED IN
THE U.K. OR N.I.

"I'm okay," Natalie assured him. But she had no idea if that was true. She was shaking from head to toe. Plus, it wouldn't hurt for both of them to be checked. Just to make sure that the smoke hadn't done any damage.

And she prayed it hadn't.

"It won't take long for the police to get here," Rick relayed to her.

There was something in the undertone of his voice that caused Natalie's pulse to quicken.

"Because this was arson," he insisted. "And because I'm almost certain that whoever set that fire was trying to kill us."

BECAUSE Rick couldn't sit still and because he couldn't go anywhere, he paced across Natalie's kitchen while he waited on hold for the police sergeant to come on to the line.

Things were going from bad to worse.

Well, in one respect. Natalie and he still weren't any closer to figuring out who was responsible for what had happened to them. That hadn't changed. But what had escalated was the attempt to hurt them. The SUV had merely alarmed them, but the fire. God, the fire. It could have killed them.

Someone meant business.

And Rick intended to find out who that someone was.

Natalie handed him a beer, and he mumbled a

thanks. He also noted that she had some color back in her cheeks and was slowly coming back to earth. The bath and the change of clothes had likely helped that. Her hair was still damp, and she wore a slim above-the-knee dress that was the color of ripe peaches.

Oh, and she was riled.

There was a good reason for that. Both of them were literally mad as hell. Maybe they could channel that anger into getting something accomplished. Turning this over to the police was the first step.

It was a step that Rick wished he'd taken much earlier. If he had, Natalie and the baby wouldn't have had to be exposed to that fire and smoke. To the danger. To the horrific memories.

Just thinking about that caused Rick to curse.

Natalie lifted an eyebrow, questioning his outburst, but he shook his head. She nodded, obviously understanding his frustration.

She was medically all right according to the ER doctor who'd examined her just hours earlier. That was something at least. They'd made it through this physically unscathed. Not mentally though.

"You should get some rest," Rick reminded her, sitting down in one of the kitchen chairs.

That earned him a loud huff. "You keep saying that. But you know that you should get some rest, too."

"I will, once I've finished with this call."

She folded her arms over her chest. "You don't have to lie to me."

And it was a lie. Rick had no intentions of resting until he'd spoken to both Dr. Henderson and the mysterious bartender, Brandon Stevens. Unfortunately, he hadn't been able to contact either of them. It was the same for the caterer himself. Sunday evening just didn't seem to be a good time to catch people in their offices or at their homes.

Or were these people purposely avoiding him?

That wouldn't work. He was going to find them.

Natalie gestured toward her phone. "I'll try to call Kitt again and see if she's learned anything new."

"Good." Though he knew it was a long shot. Kitt was efficient, and she would have definitely called them if she'd discovered anything. Still, he didn't stop Natalie. She probably needed a way to burn off the extra adrenaline and emotion, and this was likely her way of doing it. Besides, it would do her good to talk with her sister.

"Oh, and your head mechanic just dropped off your motorcycle," Natalie added.

He'd called Hal and asked him to do that, just in case Rick needed a vehicle. "Did you go outside?" he snapped.

Natalie reacted to that snap. Not with narrowed eyes or a huff. But with a sarcastic expression. "No. I watched from the window. Waved. Smiled."

"Sorry," Rick mumbled, knowing he had to do something soon or he was going to explode.

"You could try swimming," she suggested, obviously noticing his nervous energy. "There's also a treadmill in the workout room."

"You think that'll help?"

She shrugged. "Maybe. Or maybe you should go for a ride on your Harley."

"No way. I'm not leaving you here alone."

"If you don't do something, you're going to drive us both insane."

"That bad, huh?" he asked.

"That bad," she confirmed.

Natalie just stood looking at him. And since he didn't have anything else to do while he was on hold, he looked at her. He'd had some good ideas in his life.

That wasn't one of them.

She looked and smelled expensive. Probably the lingering scent of some special bath oil. Combined with her mussed, wet hair and curve-hugging dress, it gave other bad ideas of how he could burn off some of this dangerous energy.

Natalie must have sensed what he was thinking because she shifted slightly. What she didn't do was walk away, and that was something she should have done, because he wanted nothing more than to reach over, drag her into his arms…

Heck, who was he kidding?

He wanted her naked on the kitchen table. Or on the floor. He wasn't particular about the specific location. Just the specific act. He wanted to…

"This is Sergeant Garrett O'Malley," Rick heard the officer say.

It was the jolt back to reality that Rick urgently needed. He cleared his throat, took a deep breath and turned his attention away from Natalie so he could concentrate on the call.

"Sorry to keep you waiting, but I was giving a situation report to my lieutenant," the officer explained.

"And I hope that situation report identifies who set fire to my shop."

"No. It's a little too soon for that. We just started the investigation. However, judging from the preliminary evidence, we'll be calling in the fire inspectors because it does look like a case of arson. Sloppy arson at that."

"What do you mean?" Rick asked.

"There were liberal amounts of gasoline poured around both your front and back entrances. Someone apparently tossed on a couple of matches."

Gasoline and matches. Anyone could have easily acquired those. Coupled with the "sloppy" technique, that probably meant this firestarter was an amateur. Not that the end result was any less destructive. Most of his shop had been totally destroyed, and it would be weeks or even months before he could reopen for business. He didn't want to think about all the equipment and motorcycles that had been reduced to ashy rubble.

"No one in the neighborhood saw this arsonist pouring the gasoline?" Rick asked.

"We're canvassing the area, but it doesn't look good. Most of the businesses around there are closed because it's Sunday. There's an apartment building just a block up. We'll talk to everyone who lives there. We might get lucky."

Might. But the sergeant didn't sound hopeful. Rick didn't feel so hopeful, either. He tried to force that particular feeling aside. He had to stay positive. He had to stay focused. Because there was no other alternative.

When he heard another call coming through, Rick ended his conversation with the sergeant and took it.

"Rick. It's me—Kitt."

At that exact moment Natalie came back into the kitchen. She was shaking her head and mumbling something about not being able to get in touch with Kitt.

Oh, man.

This couldn't be good. Especially if Kitt had avoided talking with her sister only to call him.

Rick braced himself for more bad news. "I'm here," he let Kitt know.

"And so is Natalie, I assume?"

"Yep."

"Okay. So, here's the deal. I'll tell you what I have to tell you, and you somehow soften the blow when you pass it on to her. And before you give me a lecture about how tough Natalie is, I already know that. I also know this baby is important to her, and I don't want to do anything to put her pregnancy at risk."

Hell. This really must be bad.

"I'm listening," Rick prompted.

But that prompt also alerted Natalie. With an inquisitive look on her face, she walked toward him.

"Who is it?" Natalie mouthed.

Uh-oh. He could go two ways with this. He could lie to Natalie, but it would almost certainly come back to bite him in the butt. Lies usually did. But if he told her the truth—that her sister was on the phone and wanted him to play buffer—Natalie would no doubt want to hear the "unsoftened" version of Kitt's news.

So, this was a rock and a hard place.

Rick had a ten-second debate with himself during which time Natalie continued to ask who was on the phone and Kitt continued to ask if he was still there. He ignored both of them and went with his gut. And his gut told him that Natalie and he were a team right now, and that she was indeed strong enough to endure whatever news Kitt was about to deliver.

He hoped.

"It's your sister," Rick informed her, and before Natalie could even insist, he pressed the speaker function and placed his phone on the table so that both of them could hear the conversation.

And the first thing he heard was Kitt's rather loud huff—obviously voicing her disapproval that he hadn't kept Natalie out of this particular loop.

"Kitt, what's going on? I've been trying to reach you," Natalie explained.

"Yeah, I know. I got your messages, but I waited to call, well, because basically I didn't want to tell you this over the phone."

Natalie made a sound of contemplation. "So, you called Rick instead so you could tell him?"

Oh, yeah. Natalie was strong enough to do this.

"Put your claws back in," Kitt grumbled. "I figured I'd tell Rick, and he could pass it on to you."

"No. What you figured was that because I'm pregnant I'm somehow incapable of dealing with anything stressful or shocking. Trust me, Kitt, after what Rick and I have been through, there's nothing you can say that would compete with nearly dying in a fire."

Rick was proud of her and that famous Natalie Sinclair backbone, but he also heard the silence from Kitt. Definitely not a good sign. This was going to be really bad. So, he caught onto Natalie's hand and pulled her into the chair next to him.

That earned him a frown from Natalie. Probably because she thought he was questioning her mental strength as well. He wasn't. He figured they both might need some comforting before this was over.

"Okay, let me warn you up front that I don't have any good news. It all sucks," Kitt commented. "So, I'm just going to lay it out there and let you two deal with it." She paused just a heartbeat. "Macy's missing."

That was one of the last things he thought he would hear Kitt say. "What do you mean, she's missing?"

"I mean she left the hospital while I was at her

house getting some of her things. No one, including me, knows where she is. That makes her a missing person. I've already called the police."

"Oh, God," Natalie mumbled.

Rick slid his arm around her and pulled her to him. Natalie didn't burst into tears or anything. She took a deep breath and stared at the phone.

"When exactly did Macy leave the hospital?" Natalie wanted to know.

"The staff doesn't know for certain, but it's their best guess that she left shortly after lunch."

So, she'd been missing for hours. Kitt probably hadn't told them sooner because she'd been trying to find Macy.

"You're not going to like this next part, either," Kitt continued. "Macy had a visitor an hour before she disappeared."

"Not Dr. Benjamin?" Rick protested.

"Nope. It was the other nutso—Dr. Isabella Henderson."

"You think Dr. Henderson talked her into leaving?" Natalie asked, then turned to face Rick, alarm in her eyes. Rick figured there was alarm in his eyes, too, especially if what Dr. Benjamin had told them about Dr. Henderson was true.

"I don't know Isabella Henderson's role in all of this yet," Kitt explained. "I will, just give me a little more time to find out. There are surveillance videos, and I'm reviewing them now." Another pause. A heavy intake of breath. "But I do know that the shrink got back some of Macy's preliminary test results, and someone has been drugging the daylights out of her."

Rick mumbled "Oh, God," right along with Natalie. "What kind of drugs?"

"Mood-altering stuff available only through prescriptions. And the black market. I've got the names of them written down, and they're impossible to pronounce, but I plan to research them. It's possible Macy's been taking them voluntarily. Or not."

Rick figured it was the *or not*. However, the drugs perhaps explained Macy's recent memory problems and maybe even her bizarre behavior. But the question was—if it hadn't been voluntary, then who had given her the drugs?

Dr. Benjamin?

Maybe even Dr. Isabella Henderson?

"You were right," Natalie said to her sister. "That's a lot of bad news. Mom was drugged. Now, she's missing—"

"Oh, there's more, a lot more," Kitt interrupted. "We're having a red-letter day of joy and laughter. Troy packed up and moved out of Macy's house. Mom left a letter for him at the hospital. It was definitely Macy's handwriting, and she told Troy he was fired and that he was to leave her house immediately."

Too bad Macy hadn't left her daughters a letter to tell them where she was. Still, Rick was pleased that Troy was gone.

"Troy was apparently feeling chatty while he was packing his body buffing oil, and he whined like a baby to anyone on the staff who'd listen," Kitt explained. "His number one whine? That Rick and you are responsible for Macy firing him."

"Why did he think that?" Rick asked.

"Because in the letter Mom told him that's why she was firing him—because she thought he'd done some bad things to Natalie and you. Well, Troy didn't like the accusation and said you guys had been telling lies so that you could turn Macy against him. He threatened both of you and said payback was going to be a bitch. I excluded some other expletives, but you get the point."

"Payback," Natalie mumbled.

And Rick immediately knew what she was thinking. "When exactly did Troy move out?"

"Late last night. And here's the kicker—no one has seen him since. He's not even answering his pager or cell phone. I tried because I wanted to ask him if he'd seen Macy. That cell phone and pager are like Troy's masculine appendages. He wouldn't stop answering them unless…well, you can take your pick. He's either licking his wounds over being fired, or he's out there plotting a way to get his revenge against the two of you."

Of course, there was one other option. Troy had already tried to get revenge, that he had been the one to set the fire. Maybe Troy had been the one who tried to kill them. And if so, that likely meant he was trying to figure out how to go after them again.

"We need to find him," Rick insisted.

"Yeah. We do. I'm working on it." And judging from Kitt's somber tone, she fully understood the implications. "In the meantime, you keep Natalie safe. Hear me? Lock the doors, turn on the security alarms and *keep her safe.*"

"I will," Rick promised.

He only hoped it was a promise he could keep.

Chapter Ten

Natalie wished for a glass of chilled pinot grigio, but since alcohol and pregnancy didn't mix, she settled for some chocolate malted milk that she located in the fridge. Kitt's stash, obviously. But Natalie helped herself to it and hoped it would settle her stomach.

"Troy," Rick grumbled while he drank his beer. The longneck bottled brew was also Kitt's stash. "I wish I had five minutes alone with that SOB."

Natalie wished the same thing. Her mother's former personal assistant might have some role in all of this, and unfortunately, he was nowhere to be found so they could grill him.

Lately, that was the story of their lives.

She sat down in the chair across from him and met his troubled gaze. "Kitt will find Macy and Troy."

Rick nodded, and he sat there a moment just staring at her. "For the record, I'm moving in here with you until things settle down."

Judging from his take-no-prisoners expression, he was ready to do battle with her if she objected.

"Relax. If you hadn't suggested it, I would have." She sampled the milk, decided that it tasted far better than she'd thought it would and had a hearty sip. "I'm not an idiot, and the truth is—Kitt is going to be tied up with other things so I can't rely on her for help. And I really don't want to do this on my own. Besides, as you pointed out, you're good at kicking some serious butt."

"Yeah. And I wouldn't mind doing a little butt-kicking. It'd burn off some of this restless energy in a way that swimming and treadmills never could."

Oh, yes. He was restless all right. In the half hour since Kitt's call, Rick had raged like a storm through the house. Checking locks on windows and doors. Setting security systems. Double-checking everything. All the while grumbling and snarling.

Natalie totally understood his frustration. In addition to numerous roadblocks, fruitless calls and seemingly endless bad news, they were also going to have to live together.

It was necessity, she understood that, too. But she was under no illusions that this would be easy.

Nope.

The attraction and growing camaraderie between them was almost as dangerous as that fire had been.

She'd noticed the way Rick had looked at her earlier, before Kitt's bad-news call. And Natalie was reasonably sure that Rick had noticed the way she was looking at him.

Lustfully.

Yes, that was the only word for it. For some reason, she just kept thinking about him.

She blamed that on his jeans.

Great-looking, faded not by fashion but through frequent wear and washing. They fitted his butt to a T.

And she was so sorry she'd noticed that.

"I figured I'd hear a list of house rules by now," he commented.

"No rules." But she rethought that. In light of their long, smoldering looks and her raunchy thoughts about his jeans, there had to be at least one rule. "Well, except for kissing. We can't kiss."

Rick immediately waved that off. "Don't bother putting that off-limits. We're brainless when it comes to each other. Kissing, included."

She couldn't disagree with that. But she couldn't ignore or disagree with reality, either. "So, how do we come to terms with it and the promise we made to David?"

"We don't. We just keep trying to resist each other." He paused. "And because we're human, we'll keep failing."

His in-your-face honesty surprised her a little, though she didn't know why. There weren't many barriers left between them. That meant it was time for her to change the subject. It was the only chance they had of making it through this.

"Thank you for not treating me like a wimp," she said.

"Oh, you mean because I didn't let Kitt filter the bad news through me. You're tough as nails, Natalie. You don't need a filter."

She was glad he believed that, but she no longer felt so tough. "Actually, I just feel vulnerable."

He finished off his beer. "If you didn't feel that way, I'd be shocked. You've been through a lot in the past forty-eight hours."

She thought about that. Nodded. "Maybe that's why the attraction has snowballed."

"Maybe." He stood so he could put the bottle in the recycling bin. "That's as good a reason as any."

With restlessness still evident in his eyes and body language, he walked to the CD system mounted beneath one of the cabinets and turned it on. He made a sound of approval when a sultry Trisha Yearwood song began to play.

"Kitt's music?" he asked.

"Mine."

Rick flexed his eyebrows. "*You* listen to country music?"

"On occasion." And because she felt the need to defend herself, she added. "Hey, I'm a Texan."

"You're highbrow."

"No. I'm not. Just because I own an antique business, doesn't make me highbrow."

"Living here like this does."

"Am I going to have to defend my lifestyle?" she asked stiffly.

"Nope. And I won't have to defend mine."

"Why would you have to anyway? You're a successful business owner. There's nothing to defend."

"That sounds like a compliment." He came back toward her, slowly, without breaking eye contact. There was no more restlessness in his expression. But there was some dark, edgy emotion that she didn't want to identify.

"It *is* a compliment. We don't have to be hostile towards each other, Rick."

She blinked when he took the little plastic jug of milk from her hand and set it on the table. She blinked again when he caught onto her and eased her to a standing position.

"Come here. Dance with me."

It took her a moment to realize he was serious. "No way. Remember that part about us being brainless. We get within ten feet of each other and we start kissing."

And, simply put, Natalie didn't know if she'd stop the next time.

"Either we dance, or we continue to sit at that table and go nuts," he reminded her, motioning for her to come to him. "No kissing. Promise."

She didn't believe him, but she suddenly didn't

care. For just a moment, she wanted to feel the safety of his arms. And there was indeed safety there. Danger, too, but she decided it was worth the risk. Or maybe it was true—she was incapable of making wise choices when she got around Rick.

Natalie stepped into his arms to begin the dance.

Rick pulled her even closer, and he took the lead. Of course. She hadn't expected otherwise. He moved her into the rhythm of the smoky song. It didn't take her long to settle in, so to speak.

Natalie lowered her head, and her cheek brushed against his.

"Sorry. I didn't shave," Rick apologized.

"I don't mind. It makes you look a little like a desperado, and it goes well with your bad-boy image." Which led her to something that'd been on her mind for years. "Do you have any tattoos?"

"Why?"

"Idle curiosity."

His frown conveyed his skepticism.

"Okay. It's more than idle curiosity," she confessed. "Kitt and I used to speculate about it when we were teenagers. She figured you for a butt tat. I figured you for an arm man. I seem to recall we have a bet on it."

"How much?"

"I think it was five dollars." Except she didn't have to think. She knew it was five bucks. If pressed, Natalie could probably recall the year and the month they'd made such a wager.

More frowning, and he shook his head. "I had no idea you two would discuss something like that."

Natalie felt herself blush. Kitt and she had discussed far more than tattoos. Rick had been the subject of many of their teenage fantasies.

"So, which is it—do you have a butt or arm tattoo?" Natalie pressed.

"Right shoulder."

She smiled. "I win. I was at least in the right general vicinity. Kitt was way off."

He chuckled, his chest moving against her breasts. The sensation curled through her. A bad sensation. And Natalie eased away from him.

Rick eased her right back to him.

"I said no kissing," he reminded her. "And I meant it. Our lips will never touch."

Obviously. Because he didn't look down at her when he said that, and he kept his mouth at a reasonable distance from hers. She couldn't say the same for their bodies. No reasonable distance there.

They were touching.

She was about to remind him this wasn't a good idea, but then she felt something on her cheek. No desperado stubble this time. It was his breath, and it seemed to caress her. Of course, that was probably her imagination.

What wasn't her imagination was that they moved even closer. Natalie couldn't say who was responsible for that; it just happened.

Rick made the next thing happen though. He moved slightly so that his nose and mouth were against her hair. It seemed intimate, and it caused all kinds of alarms to go off in her head.

"You need to relax," he said, his voice low and smoky like the music.

Oh, so that's what this was all about. Not foreplay. Not torture. His attempt to get her to relax. For the sake of the baby, no doubt.

It was working.

Sort of.

Natalie could almost feel her muscles loosening. But other parts of her were all too aware that she was in a body lock with Rick. It didn't help when he moved his clever fingers along the small of her back. Small, slow, deliberate circles. Like a massage.

An erotic one.

She could feel his heartbeat against her breast. It was racing. Or maybe that was hers. Natalie could no longer tell where her body ended and his began.

Rick was true to his word. He didn't kiss her. But his breath did. It moved against her skin as his fingers worked their magic. But those fingers became even more magical when he eased his hand between them to cup her breast.

"I'm not kissing you," he said. He repeated it even as he swiped his thumb over her erect nipple.

Natalie lost her breath and suddenly didn't care if she ever found it. That touch ignited a fire inside her.

A blazing one. And her body automatically went in search of something more.

Rick gave her more.

He pressed harder against her. No random body placement, either. He slid his arm back around her waist and used it to lift her slightly so that she could feel his erection. And Natalie felt it all right. Worse, she wanted more of it.

All of it.

All of Rick.

He lowered his mouth to her ear. "I won't kiss you. Just relax."

"I can't relax. We're making out in my kitchen."

"We're dancing," he reminded her.

"It's foreplay."

"No." He stopped and eased her against the counter. "This is foreplay."

She didn't have time to question what he meant by that. His hand left her breast and slid down her body. Touching her all along the way and making her hotter than anything she could have ever imagined. Mercy, she wanted him.

He caught onto her dress, and she didn't stop him when that hand began to make its way up her thigh.

"We can't have sex," Natalie heard herself say though she had no idea how she managed something as complex as human speech.

"We're not going to have sex."

"No, we're not."

Natalie hated that she felt so disappointed, but that particular feeling was quickly replaced by the jolt of pleasure that came when he slid a hand into her panties.

"What do you like?" he asked. He was gentle. Slow. And by the time he eased his fingers into her, Natalie could only stand there and take everything he was giving her.

She shook her head. "This."

"There's more. We can just play. Just have a few minutes of fun. How about I talk dirty to you?" And he tested out a few hot suggestions that made her hotter. Wetter. She moved her hips forward, thrusting herself against his fingers.

"So, you like dirty talk," he concluded since she'd apparently lost her ability to speak. "How about this?"

He touched his mouth to that little place just below her ear. Mercy, it was sensitive. Natalie had no idea just how much until he bit gently and ran his tongue over her skin. She might have taken a moment to savor that particular sensation if the center of her body weren't begging for release.

His hand, his fingers, those insistent strokes were maddening. Rick continued with the tongue touches beneath her ear. He continued to shove his body into hers so that the pressure and the pleasure were unbearable.

Natalie didn't even bother to try to hang on. She gave in to his touch. She let herself go, and the world was suddenly a fireball. Blazing. And she came in a flash, her focus pinpointed on him.

Rick caught onto her when her legs gave way, and he held her until she returned to earth. Natalie was suddenly aware of her racing breath, her pounding heart and her sweat-dampened body.

She was also aware of what she'd just done.

Oh, mercy.

What had she just done?

"Now, you can really relax," Rick said, his mouth still against her ear.

That created a jolt of a different kind. Not a good kind, either. "Please don't tell me that was a pity orgasm because I'm pregnant with your baby."

He pulled back far enough to give her a flat look. "Trust me, I wasn't thinking about the pregnancy when I had my hand in your panties. I was thinking about hauling you onto the counter, unzipping my jeans and sinking hard and deep into you. And the pity part—not a chance. I don't have pity on my mind right now."

And to prove his point, he moved his hand and gave her an eye-crossing nudge with his erection.

"Oh," she mumbled.

"Yes, oh. Glad we could clear that up. Now, you can finish your milk and get some rest."

It seemed a nice tidy ending to something that had been far from tidy. But he was wrong about one thing. That orgasm didn't help her relax. It only made her want to go back and finish that counter and unzipped jeans scenario.

She wanted the dirty talk.

She wanted sex on the counter.

She wanted sex with Rick.

Natalie tried to hide what she was thinking, but she obviously failed miserably.

"No, you don't," Rick warned. "I know that look, and we're not going to do anything about it."

That sounded like a challenge. Okay. It only sounded that way because she was still aroused. Way too aroused. The orgasm had only whetted her appetite for something much, much more.

"I could put my hand in your jeans," she suggested. "It'll help you relax."

He gave her another flat look. "I seriously doubt that. Sex—at least the kind of sex I have in mind— isn't very relaxing. Exhausting, yes. Time-consuming, that too. But not relaxing."

Natalie clamped her teeth over her bottom lip so she wouldn't say something stupid like prove it.

But the clamping wasn't necessary. She didn't get a chance to say anything, suggestive or otherwise. The phone rang, the sound shooting through the room. Since Natalie didn't want to move fully out of Rick's embrace, she reached over to the counter and pressed the speakerphone.

"This is Dr. Isabella Henderson," the caller announced. "I believe you want to see me."

Rick and she untangled themselves from each other. Once Natalie got past the initial jolt of surprise, she was ready for a breath of relief. Rick and she obviously needed to speak to the woman, and the woman had come to them.

"What can I do for you?" Natalie asked.

"Well, for starters you can open your front door and let me in."

That brought Natalie fully out of Rick's arms, and the breath of relief was gone. She looked at Rick. He was already shaking his head and sporting a nasty scowl. He hurried to the window and glanced out.

"Dr. Henderson is standing outside by her car," Rick relayed to Natalie. Then, in a louder voice, he aimed a question at Dr. Henderson. "What do you want?"

"I think that's obvious—we need to talk."

"And just why can't we do that over the phone?" Rick demanded.

"Because I think you'll want to talk face to face when I explain who wants you dead."

Chapter Eleven

Well, this was one way to put an end to the tender moment that Natalie and he were sharing.

And it wasn't necessarily a good way to end it, either—even though they certainly needed something to end it.

Rick put the phone on Mute and stared at Natalie. She was obviously as surprised with this visit as he was.

His first instinct was to call the police and have them take Dr. Henderson in for questioning. But that instinct was slightly overpowered by his need for immediate answers and information that Dr. Henderson might have.

Might being the operative word.

Of course, seeing her was not without risks, especially if she was the person responsible for everything that had happened to Natalie and him.

He took the gun from his jacket, which he'd draped over the back of a chair. "I'll meet with her.

You go upstairs to your room and lock the door. I'll let you know when it's safe to come out."

Natalie folded her arms over her chest, and what was left of that rosy glow of passion evaporated. "You really think she came out here to kill us?"

"I don't know what to think, but I know I don't want to take any unnecessary chances."

"Part of me greatly appreciates that." Her voice mellowed. "But the other part of me doesn't think much of that idea."

"And why not?"

"For one, if she's here to hurt us, then she could just shoot you the moment you open the door. Then, she'd come after me, and I don't think a locked bedroom door would stop a bullet."

Rick agreed with part of that. The doctor probably wouldn't just come in with guns blazing. But the blazing might happen later, after she'd gained entry. And Natalie could still be hurt in such an encounter.

"So, we don't meet with her," Rick countered. "I'll call the cops."

Natalie shook her head. "If you do that, we might lose the opportunity to get to the truth because she probably won't hang around long if we don't let her in. She especially won't wait if she knows we've called the police."

"By calling the police, we might avoid the opportunity to get ourselves killed," he reminded her.

"I honestly don't think Dr. Henderson would come here to do that."

True. If the doctor was guilty, she likely wouldn't have called to announce her presence.

Well, maybe.

Maybe Isabella Henderson had counted on them feeling that way, and maybe this was a ploy to establish a false sense of security. In other words, this could be an ambush. Still, he had to make a decision, and any decision had to include Natalie's safety.

"Okay. We'll talk to her," Rick informed her. "But you stay on the other side of the room. I'll keep my gun aimed at her so she won't be inclined to make a wrong move."

"No disagreements this time. If I had a gun, I'd aim it at her as well."

Finally, they were on the same page. Rick only hoped it wasn't a page he'd regret.

Once Natalie was in place by the bar and far away from where he planned to talk to the doctor, Rick went to the door and opened it. He came face to face and eye to eye with Dr. Isabella Henderson. Petite, she wasn't. She was the same height as he was, and she wore her fifty-plus years extremely well. She wasn't flamboyant or flashy like Macy, even though the women were very close to the same age. Instead, the doctor was the picture of sophistication and professionalism with her tan business suit, pinned-up auburn hair and minimal makeup. Looking at her, it was hard for Rick to believe this woman had murder on her mind.

But he wasn't about to declare her innocent just yet.

Natalie stayed back as he'd instructed her to, and Rick moved slightly to the side so the doctor could enter.

Dr. Henderson eyed Rick's gun. "You're concerned about safety. I understand."

"Do you?" Rick fired back.

"I do. I know how difficult it must have been for you to decide to see me. Thank you."

Rick motioned for her to come into the living room. He also took her purse and plopped it on the table in the entry. Just in case she had a weapon in there, he didn't want her to have easy access to it.

The doctor's only reaction to the purse removal was a soft sigh. Other than that, she cooperated, taking a seat in the living room, and she placed her hands in her lap. "Dr. Benjamin told me about your situation and the conversation he had with you."

"Did he also tell you that he accused you of some assorted felonies?" Rick asked.

"No. But I suspected as much. That's yet another reason for us to talk. So I can explain my side of the story."

Rick shrugged. "So, start explaining."

"Well, for one thing—I didn't drug you so you'd impregnate Natalie with a phase-two baby. I've given up on the Cyrene Project."

None of this was a surprise, but Rick continued with the questions. He also glanced at Natalie to make sure she was staying put. She was. "Why did you give up on it?"

"Simply put, my interests lie elsewhere—with genetic memory research. I don't have time for something as inconsequential as Dr. Benjamin's passé ideas about eugenics."

It was time for Rick to go for the jugular. "Funny, he said you were scared that the medical community would learn of your involvement and that you might lose funding for your latest research."

"Nonsense." She said it calmly enough, but it was a sore point. For a moment, just a moment, the anger flashed in her eyes. "I'm a successful researcher in my own right, and I'm not in danger of losing funding."

"So, why would Benjamin lie?"

"To take suspicion off himself. The truth is—there's only one person I know of who'd want a phase-two baby, and that's Dr. Benjamin himself."

"And what about the other side to this—who's trying to kill us?" Natalie didn't wait for the doctor to answer. "Because if Dr. Benjamin is truly obsessed about this baby I'm carrying, then he couldn't possibly want us dead. You, on the other hand, might want that."

Rick gave Natalie a nod of approval. The accusation was dead-on.

"Why would I possibly want to harm you?" Dr. Henderson responded.

Natalie had a quick answer. "Perhaps because you're jealous that Dr. Benjamin succeeded, and you want to do some serious harm to the Cyrene Project?"

The doctor had an equally quick denial. "That's absurd."

"Is it?" Natalie fired back.

Oh, that brought on slightly more than a flash of anger. The doc was fighting hard to keep control of what appeared to be a nasty temper.

"Accusing me of attempted murder is absurd," the doctor insisted. "And don't be so hasty in declaring Dr. Benjamin innocent of trying to kill you. Did he tell you that he's concerned about an upcoming federal investigation into his unethical research?"

Now, she'd managed to surprise him. Rick shook his head. "No."

"I didn't think so. He found out three days ago, and that's why I severed our relationship. Our friendship. The investigation could close down the Cyrene Project permanently, and it could even earn him some jail time."

"You mean because of the drugging?" Rick asked.

The doctor nodded. "That, and some other coercion tactics that he'd prefer the authorities not learn about."

Rick followed that through to its conclusion. Dr. Benjamin could have been the one who drugged them. And after he learned about the investigation into the Cyrene Project, he could also be the one who tried to kill them—so he could eliminate anyone who could testify against him.

Of course, Dr. Henderson could be lying.

"Do you have any proof about Dr. Benjamin's coercion tactics or any other illegal activity?" Natalie asked their guest.

"No. The computer files and hard copies I had regarding the Cyrene Project mysteriously disappeared on the same day we learned about the upcoming investigation."

She seemed riled about that. Rick understood completely. He was still incensed that someone had stolen his lab tests.

"There's also the possibility that Dr. Benjamin is innocent," Dr. Henderson concluded.

He studied her a moment, trying to figure out why she'd let her former partner off the hook when she was the one who'd put him there just moments earlier. "Then if he's innocent, that brings us back to you."

"Or it brings us back to someone else who might have a vested interest in the Cyrene Project." The doctor turned her attention to Natalie. "Like your mother's personal assistant, for instance."

Troy again. Rick was getting awfully tired of hearing the man's name emerge every time suspects were named. Though he had to admit that by disappearing, Troy wasn't doing anything to make himself look innocent or to clear his name. Just the opposite.

"I went to the hospital to visit your mother," the doctor continued. "But I understand she left without informing anyone of her whereabouts. My advice is to find her and have her institutionalized. In my opinion Macy is in need of long-term intensive therapy."

Rick glanced at Natalie. She looked concerned over that last suggestion so Rick moved the conversation along.

"The police will no doubt want to talk to you," he informed Dr. Henderson.

She took a deep breath, but that was her only reaction to what had to have been unsettling news. "I suspected as much. I'll deal with that when the time comes." She stood and faced Rick. "And what about you? Could you live with the arrest of someone you love?"

Rick quickly went back through the conversation to see if he'd missed anything. "What do you mean?"

No flash of anger, but her mouth relaxed into a smug half smile. "I was talking about your uncle Carlton."

Rick was sure he blinked. "Carlton? What does he have to do with this?"

"Maybe everything."

"Are we supposed to understand what that means?" Natalie asked.

The smugness went up a significant notch. "I'm sure you know that Carlton doesn't approve of this pregnancy. He's always been vehemently opposed to Dr. Benjamin's research—especially since it cost him your mother, the woman he loved, the woman he considered to be his soul mate."

"And you're saying…?" Rick stopped with that. Because he didn't even want to speculate where the doctor was going with this accusation.

"I'm saying Carlton will do just about anything to stop the Cyrene Project. *Anything*. My advice? If you're looking for a would-be killer, look in his direction."

NATALIE WAS more than happy to usher Dr. Isabella Henderson out of the house. She'd been eager to talk to the doctor, eager to get any information, but that information had come at a high price.

She'd all but accused Rick's Uncle Carlton of arson and attempted murder.

Rick was trying to handle the news well. He was pulling his stoic routine. Silence. Staring off into space. The occasional pacing.

It wasn't working.

Natalie could see the tension building inside him. It was like watching a volcano about to erupt.

She followed him into the living room where he was presently pacing and tried to figure out the best way to do some damage control. She decided to go with the simple approach.

"Dr. Henderson could be lying about Carlton," she pointed out.

"Maybe." He stopped pacing and went to the window to look out. "But the pieces fit."

"No, they don't. Carlton loves you, and despite how he feels about Dr. Benjamin or me, he wouldn't try to kill you."

She prayed that was true, but Natalie wasn't even sure she could be objective about the truth. Both Carlton and her mother's assistant, Troy, had been implicated, but those implications had come from two people who also had motives to hurt Rick and her.

Isabella Henderson and Claude Benjamin.

Dr. Benjamin could be after them to eliminate the phase-two baby he'd wanted, since that particular baby could now also be the physical evidence to send him to jail. Of course, Dr. Henderson could want them out of the way to preserve her reputation and funding.

Still, she couldn't totally discount that Carlton wasn't involved. She just hoped that involvement was one that wouldn't spur a criminal prosecution.

Rick bracketed his hands on each side of the window and kept his back to her. He probably didn't realize how powerful and brooding he was just standing there. Natalie also noted that he was hot and sexy, but since it was a totally inappropriate thought, she kept it to herself. However, after the near-counter incident, the dirty talk and the orgasm, she figured she'd have to suppress a lot more thoughts like those.

"Carlton was at the motorcycle shop just before the fire started," Rick reminded her.

Yes. And that disturbed her as well. It also disturbed her that Carlton had stormed out in a fit of anger. "Still, that proves nothing."

"It proves he had the opportunity and the means. We already know what his motive might be." Rick groaned and then cursed softly. He turned around to face her, leaning his back against the wall. "When my parents were killed five years ago, Carlton was there for me. He's the only family I have left." He glanced at her stomach. "Well, except for the baby."

Yes, she was lucky in that respect. She had Kitt and her brother, Wyatt. And her mother…wherever she was.

And the baby, of course.

This baby had become the impetus for her to keep her composure. After all, screaming from frustration probably wouldn't be good for the pregnancy.

Natalie walked toward him. "It's strange. Even with everything that's happened, I'm beginning to understand just how much this baby means to me."

"Same here," Rick agreed.

"Really?" And Natalie hated that she sounded so surprised.

Rick shrugged. "I've always wanted kids, but I'd given up on love and marriage."

"Yes." Because of what had happened with David. "Me, too."

He reached for her, and as if it were the most natural thing in the world, he pulled her into his arms. He smelled good. Like soap and shampoo, probably from the shower he'd taken after they'd returned from the fire.

"Yet, here we are," he continued. "Eight months away from being parents."

"Eight months," Natalie repeated, suddenly feeling the enormity of it all. "Seems a little over-whelming, doesn't it?"

"Sometimes. It won't be easy to work out things between us."

She thought about that and knew that wasn't exactly true. They were already working things out. They were already on the same side. Holding each other, at that. And the shared concern and camarade-rie seemed to be growing by leaps and bounds.

Natalie leaned her head against his shoulder before she even realized she was doing it. She was settling into his embrace, taking comfort from him.

And that was a mistake.

She stepped away from him, and Rick gave her a puzzled stare. "It was just a hug. Nothing more."

"Yes, but we know where hugs lead, don't we? We have no willpower, Rick. Zilch. Distance is the only thing that will help us."

He just stood there and continued to look welcom-ing and, well, hot. It was all she could do to stop herself from going right back to him.

She groaned and pushed her hair away from her face. "Mercy, this is hard."

He stared at her before the corner of his mouth

lifted. A dimple flashed in his left cheek. "At times you have the same effect on me."

"Don't smile," she warned. "Those dimples are lethal weapons and you know it."

"You like dimples?"

"I like *your* dimples," she admitted. Natalie immediately wanted to throttle herself because this was verbal foreplay. No doubt about it. But then, lately, breathing seemed to be foreplay. "I just keep reminding myself that we'd feel horrible if we broke that promise to David."

"Yeah." He shoved his hands into the pockets of his jeans. "I go through the whole range of emotions. Heck, I've even gotten mad at David for making that request."

"Me, too."

It did seem a little selfish, and Natalie was immediately disgusted with herself for thinking that. David had been terribly hurt by what Rick and she had done. Added to his already fragile mental health, he certainly had a right to ask them to stay away from each other.

Now, it was up to Rick and her to fulfill that promise. Somehow.

"It'll be easier once we find the person responsible for trying to kill us," Natalie continued. "Then we won't be seeing each other every minute of every day."

It was a good rationalization, but Natalie also knew something else. That Rick being out of sight wouldn't mean he was out of mind. Something had changed between them, and they wouldn't be able to go back to they way things were.

"You're right," she heard Rick say.

Natalie pulled herself out of her thoughts. "About what?"

"Once we find out who wants us dead, then the police can arrest him or her. There'll be no reason for me to be here all the time. So, let's put this lust on the back burner and get on with it."

Natalie nodded, though she knew there'd be no putting her lust on any back burners. Thanks to the incident in the kitchen, he was firmly on her mind. Still, she needed to focus on something other than that. Something that would help them solve this riddle.

"I suppose I could call Kitt to see if she's had any luck finding Macy," Natalie suggested. But that might just interrupt her sister from doing something important. After all, if Kitt had indeed found Macy, she would have already gotten in touch.

Well, unless her sister was trying to shelter her from more bad news.

"I have a better idea," Rick said, taking out his cell phone. "I'm calling Carlton." He pressed in the number and then hit the speakerphone button. "I'm just going to ask him point-blank if he's involved in any of this."

Natalie didn't even attempt to stop him. As difficult as this conversation would be, it needed to happen if only so it would help rid Rick of any doubts about his uncle.

Now, the question was—how could Natalie rid herself of her own doubts about Carlton?

She silently admitted that she had reservations about the man, mainly because he disliked her so much. Still, that wasn't a reason for murder.

She listened to the sound of the phone ringing at Carlton's house. No answer for the first five, and she figured his answering machine would soon kick in.

It didn't.

On the sixth ring, someone picked up.

But that person didn't utter any sort of greeting. There was just an eerie silence.

"Carlton?" Rick said. "Are you there?"

The silence continued for several seconds. "No. Carlton's not here right now. I don't know where he is."

Natalie had no trouble recognizing that voice, but she did have trouble figuring out why she was hearing that particular voice from Carlton's phone. "Mom?"

"It's me," Macy confirmed.

Okay. That was the one person she hadn't expected to be there. "What are you doing at Carlton's house?"

"I came to see him, but he's not home."

Rick and Natalie exchanged uneasy glances. "Stay put. I'll be there in fifteen minutes," Natalie insisted.

"No," was her mother's response.

"No?" Natalie challenged. "Mom, be reasonable. We have to talk. You need help."

"I don't need your kind of help. You tried to have me locked up in the psych ward. I'm not crazy."

"I know you're not. Someone's been drugging you, and we need to find out who's doing that. Just stay there, and Rick and I will come and get you."

"No. It's too late for that. Much too late. I have to do something to stop this."

"What do you mean?" And Natalie actually held her breath, waiting to hear an explanation.

But Macy didn't answer. She mumbled something that Natalie couldn't distinguish and hung up.

Chapter Twelve

While he waited for Kitt to phone him back, Rick
fixed Natalie a grilled cheese sandwich and coaxed
her into eating. She balked, of course. And then she
balked about not doing more to help find her mother.

Rick understood her frustration. He, too, second-
guessed his decision to send Kitt to Carlton's house
to look for Macy. Rick would have preferred to do
that task himself. But if he did that, it would mean
leaving Natalie alone. She wouldn't have eaten, she
wouldn't have rested, and the worst part was that he
wouldn't have been there if something went wrong.
He couldn't put her and the baby's safety behind
finding her mother.

Kitt had felt the same way. She'd been insistent
that they stay put in Natalie's house while she hurried
to Carlton's. Kitt's insistence, however, might have
been driven by the fact that Macy apparently no
longer trusted Natalie or him. Still, Rick's second-

guessing continued until the call finally came. He snatched it up on the first ring.

"Macy's not here," Kitt informed him.

Rick gave a frustrated huff. He hadn't really expected Macy to still be at his uncle's place, not after making those troubling comments to them over the phone. No, Macy had probably left within minutes of hanging up.

"I've searched the entire house," Kitt continued. The worry in her voice was evident even over the phone. "No one, including Carlton, is here."

Rick nearly suggested that Kitt canvass the neighborhood, but that would likely be a waste of time. Even if the neighbors had seen Macy, they almost certainly wouldn't know where she was now. If she had access to a car and money—and she probably did—she could be anywhere.

"How's Natalie?" Kitt asked.

Rick looked at her. She was seated in a chair across from him. She had her feet tucked beneath her in a comfortable pose. But what ruined that facade of comfortableness was the bunched-up forehead and the lip-nibbling.

"I'm fine," Natalie assured her sister, but since she practically snarled when she said it, Rick knew she was far from fine.

"I hired a PI," Kitt continued. "Well, actually I hired an entire crew of them. They're looking for our missing trio—Macy, Troy and the bartender, Brandon Stevens."

That was a good start, and Rick knew if Kitt could find any of the three it would be a victory. Heck, anything positive at this point would be not just a victory but a miracle. "If they have any available manpower, I also want them to check into Dr. Benjamin and Isabella Henderson."

"Anything specific?" Kitt asked.

"I'd like to know if there's a possible federal investigation into the Cyrene Project. Isabella Henderson said that Dr. Benjamin learned about such an investigation three days ago. That's not long before someone started trying to kill Natalie and me."

"Well, my money's on Benjamin so I'll tell the PIs to dig extra hard when looking at him. I'll get back to you when I have something."

"Thanks, Kitt." Rick clicked off the phone and glanced at Natalie. She was stewing about something, and he didn't have to guess what. "You're upset because your sister is trying to keep you out of this?"

Natalie nodded. "She's treating me like an invalid."

"No. Kitt's treating you like a sister she loves." Still, he knew this was tough on Natalie. She was like him in so many ways, including that stubborn, do-it-myself way. This wasn't just a blow to her ego, it probably made her feel distrusted, belittled and useless.

Still, there was nothing he could do about it except keep apologizing. He couldn't risk anything happening to her or the baby. And that included safeguarding her health in general.

He checked his watch. It wasn't really that late. Barely past 8:00 p.m. But since it'd been a long, hellish day, he decided to call it a night.

"You need to get some rest." Rick stood and motioned for her to stand as well.

Natalie frowned. "That has a you're-an-invalid tone to it."

"Well, it wasn't intentional. I was aiming for an I'm-tired-and-I-can't-rest-until-you-do tone."

She couldn't argue, though he could tell that she wanted to do just that. Instead, she gave a very loud huff and followed him.

Rick had already checked the security system, the windows and doors to make sure no one could get in without setting off the alarms. He grabbed his gun that he'd left on the foyer table and headed up the stairs.

Toward Natalie's bedroom.

Rick figured he'd deliver his ultimatum once they were there.

"Maybe these PIs can find Macy," Natalie commented.

Rick knew it wasn't an idle comment, either. She was no doubt extremely concerned about her mother. Macy was disoriented, missing and possibly still drugged.

Macy could also be in danger.

Natalie had probably already figured that out as well. Because the person who wanted to kill them just might use Macy to get to them. In Macy's present state of mind, she might not realize she was being used until it was too late.

Hence, the reason he was carrying a gun, and the reason for the ultimatum he was about to deliver.

He opened Natalie's bedroom door and then turned to face her. He took a deep breath. "I'm staying in here with you tonight. And before you argue—hear me out. Security systems aren't perfect, and if something goes wrong, I don't want to be all the way down the hall. I want to be here, right next to you, so I can protect you."

Rick braced himself for another invalid argument, but it didn't come.

"So, we're sleeping together?" she concluded.

Now, why did that sound like a carnal invitation?

Probably because his dumb male body decided to interpret it that way. He told his body to knock it off. This was essentially business.

His body laughed at him.

"But I meant that only in the literal sense—as in, we'll actually be sleeping and nothing else," Rick explained. And he hoped his body grasped that tidy explanation because sleeping was the only thing that was going to happen in that bed tonight.

She folded her arms over her chest. "Is this like your no-kissing session?"

He mimicked the smart-mouthed look she was giving him. "I wish. But that kind of activity won't leave much time for rest. You're resting."

"I'm beginning to hate that word," she grumbled.

"No, you don't. You're exhausted, and getting off your feet will feel darn good. I promise."

The staring war began. It was a battle of wills. Rick knew he would win. Why? Because of those dark, sleep-starved circles beneath her eyes.

It didn't take long.

"All right, I am tired," she admitted. She dropped her arms to her sides, turned and headed for her dressing room to change for bed.

And that brought Rick to the next dilemma on his full plate of dilemmas.

Could he really sleep in the same room with Natalie and not touch her?

Since he really didn't want to examine that and since he didn't like the obvious answer that came to mind, he pushed the question aside, put his gun on the nightstand and took out his cell phone. Work was the best cure for dirty thoughts about Natalie.

He called his head mechanic, Hal, to give him an update on the fire—that it was arson and the place would likely be closed for several weeks. As Rick figured he would, Hal volunteered to call the rest of the workers and pass on the news. Rick thanked him, hung up and made the next call on his list.

To Dr. Macomb, to see if the man had located the missing lab results.

No such luck.

The results and his blood samples were nowhere to be found. They'd simply vanished.

Rick figured it was time they gave up on that particular angle. Besides, the test would have only proven what was used to drug him, not who had done the drugging.

Frustrated that he was spinning his wheels, Rick sat on the end of the chaise adjacent to the bed.

Yes, the bed.

It was the place Natalie and he had had sex. The place where he'd gotten her pregnant.

The place where they'd spend yet another night.

Lucky him.

This time though, they wouldn't be drugged, and they'd have no excuses. They would keep their hands off each other.

He repeated that.

Despite what'd happened earlier in the kitchen, that was as far as Rick could take things in the sexual, making-out department. He could rationalize that giving Natalie some much-needed release didn't totally violate the promise to David. After all, it hadn't been sex.

Though it had been pleasurable.

For Natalie. For him.

For him, it'd been torture, too, but Rick had savored that look of passion and surrender on Natalie's face. Man, pleasuring her had been the ultimate pleasure. Taking in her scent. Feeling her shatter. Hearing that erotic little hitch she made deep within her throat.

He was becoming aroused just thinking about it.

Which was the exact reason why he couldn't think about it. It was also the reason he would need a cold shower or two before this night was over.

His need for a cold shower increased significantly when Natalie came out of her dressing room.

She wore dark purple pjs and a matching robe. The fabric was silk, but other than that, it wasn't provocative. In fact, it covered as much of her body as sleepwear could cover.

Unfortunately, Rick's imagination quickly filled in the blanks.

He was betting Natalie had some very good blanks.

"You're smiling," she pointed out.

"Am I?" He immediately tried to change his expression.

She smiled, too. Briefly. It let him know that she knew what he was thinking. Damn her. The woman was a mind reader.

She tipped her head to the chaise where he was sitting. "Is that where you plan to sleep?"

He glanced back at the piece of antique furniture in question. It was rose-colored and girlie. But it would have to do. He wasn't leaving Natalie alone. "Sure."

"Now who's being stubborn?" she grumbled. "The chaise is five feet long and meant for delicate Victorian ladies. You're six foot two, not Victorian and not delicate. The bed is big enough for both of us."

It was. Probably three times larger than his own bed.

But it still wasn't big enough.

The Grand Canyon wasn't big enough when it came to Natalie and him.

"Don't you dare give me an argument about this," she said, practically glaring at him. "I've been sub-jected to invalid treatment and constant requests to rest. Well, I'm going to rest, and so are you."

Rick nearly argued with her, but he knew it was an argument he couldn't win. He didn't really want to win it, either. In addition to the chaise being more than a foot too short, it just wasn't very comfortable.

Still, the need for comfort didn't outweigh his need to keep sane. He kept on his jeans and T-shirt and only removed his boots and socks before he got onto the bed. Oh, and he stayed on top of the covers. That would put a linen-and-silk chastity belt between them.

Too bad it wasn't something much sturdier.

"We'd better get used to this," Natalie commented as she climbed into bed. She used the covers, too, pulling them all the way up to her chin. "I don't mean the bed-sharing, but we'd better get used to being around each other. When the baby comes, you'll be over here for visits."

"Yeah." And Rick was thankful that that gave him something else to think about other than being in bed with Natalie. If he'd done the math right, by early spring their baby would be born.

"It's silly, but I'm scared," she said. She rolled on

her side so he could see her. "I mean, that whole giving-birth process." She made a face.

Rick made a face, too—mainly because he thought about Natalie going through all that pain. "Maybe I can be in the delivery room with you," he offered. Not that he had a clue how that would help. Still, he left the offer on the table.

She didn't say anything right away, and he began to interpret that as a no. After all, they weren't real lovers. Definitely not partners. Yet, his being there would be the most intimate thing two people could ever experience. Then there was that whole part about her being naked. She really might object to his seeing that.

"Okay," she mumbled.

"Okay?" he questioned.

He waited until she nodded before he took it as a genuine okay. He didn't know whether to be happy or to panic. The panic was winning by a nose, but he knew this was a gift. The ultimate gift.

"But I think we have to go through classes, too," Natalie added. She hesitated and groaned. "Mercy, we're not going to be able to do this."

Because he was afraid she'd rescind her offer to let him witness the birth of his child, he stayed quiet, waiting for her to continue.

"I want you," she whispered.

Oh. So, it had nothing to do with giving birth. It was that old issue that'd been between them since they were old enough to know what sex and attraction were. It was ironic. Because of their parents' matchmaking, they'd avoided each other.

Until that night that David had walked in on them kissing.

That kiss had been a lapse, but Rick knew there'd be other lapses. Because it was true—Natalie and he were attracted to each other.

"I keep thinking that if we just have sex," Natalie continued. "I mean, one of those wild, crazy, against-the-wall kinds of sexual encounters, that whatever's between us will just burn up. That all these aches and yearnings will go away because they've been sated."

He turned on his side as well and faced her. "Sex against the wall?" And because he thought they needed some levity, he added. "That's not very original, and it's really hard on the back and legs."

It worked. She smiled a moment before she groaned. "I'm not usually this preoccupied with sex."

Neither was he. It seemed to happen any time he was around Natalie. "We could just blame the pregnancy hormones again."

She nodded. "Yes. That's good." Her gaze met his. "I'll go to sleep now."

Her eyes stayed open.

Their gazes continued to connect. Rick also continued to feel the heat simmering between them, and that sex-against-the-wall idea was gaining momentum.

"I could take the edge off for you," he suggested. "Not sex though."

Natalie actually seemed to consider that, and Rick wondered why he'd ever opened this Pandora's box in the first place. Oh. It was because he wanted her bad.

"I could take the edge off for you," she countered.

He thought maybe his eyes crossed. "I don't doubt that, but please—spare me the details of how you'd do that. Because other than torturing each other with all this edge and sex talk, nothing other than sleep is going to happen tonight."

"What about tomorrow?" she teased.

"Smart-ass."

But it was the billon-dollar question. He could keep things under control tonight because he knew Natalie was exhausted. It was the drunken-babe rule again. But tomorrow—well, that's what cold showers were for.

And apparently phones.

The phone next to her bed rang, putting on hold their discussion about sex. Rick reached over and answered it.

"It's me," Kitt greeted. "For a change of pace, are you ready for some good news?"

Rick released the breath he'd been holding. "You bet."

"I located Macy."

"Thank God." Since he couldn't find a speaker function on this particular phone, he relayed the news to Natalie and motioned for her to move closer so she could hear the conversation.

"Is Mom all right?" Natalie immediately asked. She scooted across the bed, put her face close to his and waited for her sister to respond.

"She's disoriented but not hurt. She was at her health club trying to get into the sauna while wearing street clothes, and someone on the staff called me. She refused to go back to the hospital, so I'm taking her home."

"We can be there in twenty minutes," Rick offered.

"I'd rather you stay put for an hour or two. I hate to sound rude, but it'll be easier for me to get her settled in if you're not there."

That was true—especially if Macy still believed that Natalie had tried to have her committed to a mental institution. Still, Rick wanted to be there so that Kitt wouldn't have to handle this alone.

"The doctor is on the way over to examine her," Kitt continued. "I'll make sure the place is secure. You've done the same for Natalie?"

"Of course."

"Good. Okay, here's what the PIs have learned, and that good news doesn't necessarily apply to this part. It's true about the upcoming investigation into the Cyrene Project. The feds informed Dr. Isabella Henderson and Dr. Benjamin of that less than a week ago."

So, that meant Dr. Benjamin had a motive for attempted murder. The stark look on Natalie's face was an indication that she'd realized this as well.

"According to the Justice Department agent who informed them, the doctors had a huge argument, and Isabella Henderson threatened Benjamin. It got very ugly."

Rick didn't doubt that. There was a lot at stake and not just reputations. Jail time was a possibility. Either one might be trying to cover their tracks.

"I'm thinking that one or both of them drugged us," Natalie explained. "And then one or both decided this baby shouldn't exist because it's evidence against them."

"That's what I was thinking, too," Kitt mumbled. "But there's more. The PI found out something else when he talked to the agent."

"What?" Rick asked when Kitt didn't automatically continue.

"The agent gave the PI the name of the person who tipped off the feds about the Cyrene Project. Brace yourself, Rick. It was your uncle, Carlton."

Chapter Thirteen

"I'm not sure it's a good idea for you to be out like this," Rick grumbled as he turned into the drive of her mother's estate.

Natalie heard him, but what she also noticed was that he wasn't pushing his grumbled complaint. He hadn't wanted her to go to her mother's house, but he also understood her need to see her mother, to make sure Macy was truly okay.

She in turn understood his need to make sure Carlton hadn't done something criminal. Natalie had already reassured Rick several times that Carlton wasn't a killer.

It hadn't helped.

Rick's plan was once they'd visited her mother, he would get one of the PIs to stay with Natalie while he had a little chat with his uncle.

Natalie figured that *chat* wouldn't be friendly.

"What the heck?" Rick mumbled, obviously

noticing the cars parked in the circular drive of her mother's house. "That's Dr. Henderson's car."

"You're sure?" Natalie asked.

"Yeah. I saw it when she came to visit. What would she be doing here?"

"I have no idea. Macy and she know each other well, but other than the visit to the hospital Dr. Henderson's not in the habit of making social calls."

Of course, maybe this was an impromptu visit like the one Dr. Henderson had paid to Rick and her. Maybe the doctor was still on a mission to clear her name and point the proverbial finger at Dr. Benjamin.

But Natalie had another thought. Perhaps the doctor's motive wasn't so benign and she wanted to do Macy harm.

Natalie jumped out of the car the moment that Rick parked and hurried up the steps. Rick hurried as well and easily caught up with her.

The front door was locked—probably one of Kitt's security measures—so Natalie rang the bell and waited. Impatiently waited. That impatience and concern went up a notch when she heard the voices.

Loud voices.

The people inside were arguing.

It obviously alarmed Rick because he began to pound. Natalie was sure if Kitt hadn't opened it, that Rick would have kicked in the door.

"What's going on here?" Natalie immediately asked her sister.

Kitt scowled. "Chaos."

With that vague explanation, Rick pushed past her and headed toward those voices. Natalie and Kitt hurried behind him, and Natalie soon saw what her sister had meant by chaos. Her mother was in her sitting room, but she wasn't alone. She had three visitors.

Dr. Claude Benjamin.

Dr. Isabella Henderson.

And Carlton.

"Macy called them," Kitt explained, and her tone conveyed her displeasure. "She said it was time to get a few things straight. Personally, I think it's time for Rick to start banging some heads together so they'll all shut up."

"I agree," Rick growled. He stepped into the room, and he must have garnered their attention because everyone quit arguing.

The room went silent.

"You," Rick said, pointing to Dr. Benjamin, "are leaving—*now*. You can either walk out, or I'll toss you out. Your choice. Personally, I'm hoping you opt for the toss."

"I can't leave. Not until I make Macy understand."

"I understand perfectly," Macy insisted. "You're a scheming, lying monster who drugged my daughter so she'd become pregnant."

Dr. Benjamin walked toward Macy. "I did no such thing."

"Then it was your former partner," Macy continued, volleying fiery glances between both doctors. "And if I find out which one of you did it, there'll be hell to pay. Hear that? *Hell.*"

Well, her mother certainly didn't seem drugged and disoriented, and despite the circumstances, that pleased Natalie.

"And that hell will apply to the person who was drugging Macy," Rick added. "Okay, who gets tossed first?"

And his glare included his uncle.

"I've had enough of this," Dr. Henderson snarled. "I'm warning all of you—you're looking at a lawsuit if you don't stop maligning my good name by linking it to this charlatan."

Isabella aimed a nasty glare at Claude Benjamin and headed for the door. Both Rick and Natalie watched to make sure she would indeed leave. Once she'd slammed the door behind her, they turned back to the other guests.

"I'm staying put," Carlton insisted. "We have to talk, and you know it."

Natalie knew that was true. Rick would no doubt need to hear the rationale for Carlton tipping off the feds. If Carlton's motive was to get Dr. Benjamin arrested, then it wasn't a bad thing.

She just wanted to know why he hadn't informed Rick sooner of what he'd done.

Why had Carlton kept it a secret?

"I have just one thing to say," Dr. Benjamin interjected into the tense silence. He looked at Natalie. "I would do nothing to hurt you. *Nothing.* You're like my own daughter, and I care for you."

That did nothing to reassure her he was innocent. In fact, Natalie couldn't believe a word he said.

"Time to go," Rick said, latching onto the man's arm.

Claude Benjamin didn't fight the manhandling, and he let Rick lead him to the door. But he didn't stay silent. He gave them one last parting shot. "Watch out for Troy and Dr. Henderson. They're dangerous."

Rick didn't even acknowledge the warning. He shoved the doctor outside, closed the door and double-locked it.

"Speaking of the devil, where is Troy?" Rick asked Macy.

She shook her head. "I don't know. I haven't seen him since he visited me in the hospital."

"Good. Keep it that way," Natalie insisted. "Mom, he may have been the person drugging you."

"Yes. That did occur to me—after the fact." She gave a weary sigh. "I trusted him, and he's a wolf in sheep's clothing, isn't he?" She didn't wait for them to confirm that. She spared all four of them a considering glance. "You obviously have things to discuss, and I'm exhausted. If you need me, I'll be in my room."

Kitt began to follow Macy, but Natalie caught onto her sister's arm and pulled her aside. "Can you check and make sure none of her vitamins and regular meds have been tampered with?" she whispered. "Maybe you'll be able to tell if the capsules have been opened and the contents replaced with something else."

Kitt nodded. "Sure. I'll flush them just in case Troy or whoever decided to continue their criminal activity. Now, if we can just figure out why someone would want to drug her."

Natalie could think of a reason, and it didn't necessarily involve Troy.

Dr. Benjamin could be responsible, because Macy was a vocal opponent of the Cyrene Project and this was his way of silencing her. Still, Troy could have done it simply to keep Macy under his control. Either way, her mother had become a pawn in a very dangerous game, and Natalie wasn't about to forget that. Someone would pay for what they'd done.

"Good luck," Kitt mumbled.

Natalie followed her sister's gaze to Rick and Carlton. Neither of them was saying a word, but their body language indicated they were posturing for a fight.

Great.

Just what she didn't need tonight.

"Thanks," Natalie answered, and she walked away from her sister so she could join Rick. She didn't want him to have to go through this alone—especially since Carlton's venom would almost certainly be aimed at her and not Rick.

"We learned that you're the one who contacted the authorities about the Cyrene Project," Rick said. "Why didn't you tell us you'd done that?"

There was a flash of anger in Carlton's eyes. "Because I didn't want anyone to know. Especially you," he stared at Natalie. "I'm still not convinced that you weren't in on this phase-two plan right from the beginning."

His accusation shouldn't have been a surprise, but it was. "You think I arranged to have Rick drugged so he'd sleep with me?"

"I don't think you turned down the idea when Dr. Benjamin came to you with it."

"Dr. Benjamin didn't come to Natalie or me with anything," Rick said, stepping between them. "Besides, if Natalie truly wanted a phase-two baby, all she had to do was ask Dr. Benjamin to pair her with another Cyrene Project male. She didn't need me."

"She wanted you. She still wants you."

Natalie couldn't refute that. After all, she'd confessed that to Rick less than an hour ago. But she could challenge that this was any of Carlton's business. "I don't intend to discuss my personal feelings with you."

"But I intend to ask you some questions," Rick insisted, staring at his uncle. "Did you start the fire at my shop?"

Carlton looked genuinely insulted. "I can't believe you'd ask me that."

"I can't believe you'd give me a reason to ask it, but you have. For whatever reason, you've decided to blame Natalie for everything that's happened. And you know what—I'm more than a little tired of that. So, how about an answer to my question—did you start the fire?"

"I'm not going to stand here and have you talk to me like that."

Rick stepped in front of his uncle when Carlton started to leave. "Did you start the fire?"

And Natalie held her breath. Before this conversation, before she'd seen Carlton's reaction, she'd been so certain that he was innocent. That he couldn't have possibly started the fire that nearly killed them.

But she wasn't so sure now.

"I had nothing to do with that fire," Carlton declared. But he dodged Rick's gaze, making Natalie wonder if it was an outright lie.

"Are you saying you've done nothing to Natalie and me?" Rick pressed. "Nothing other than make that call to the feds about the Cyrene Project?"

Carlton didn't answer. Nor did he look at either of them. He fixed his attention on the floor.

Oh, mercy.

For Rick's sake, she'd prayed that Carlton was innocent, but his behavior indicated otherwise.

"What did you do?" Rick demanded.

Carlton shifted his posture slightly, and he slowly

met Rick's gaze. "I did you a favor. Or rather that's what I tried to do. I knew I had to do whatever it took to keep you away from Natalie."

Natalie felt her breath stall in her throat. "What do you mean?" she asked.

But Carlton didn't address her. He aimed his response at Rick. "I mean that I spoke to David while he was in the hospital. While he lay dying in the emergency room. And I told him that Natalie and you had to stay away from each other. That if you two got together it would continue this sick Cyrene Project. David agreed. He understood what I was asking him to do, and he did it."

Rick took a step toward his uncle and got right in his face. "What did you ask him to do?"

Carlton stared defiantly into Rick's eyes. "I wanted David to make you swear that you'd never get involved with Natalie. And that's exactly what he did."

RICK DIDN'T KNOW who was more surprised by Carlton's revelation: Natalie or him. For Rick, the surprise lasted several moments.

And then the anger kicked in.

"Let me get this straight—it wasn't David's idea for Natalie and me to stay apart?"

"No," Carlton readily admitted. "In fact, David decided to kill himself so that he'd clear the way for the two of you."

Natalie walked toward Carlton. Or rather she

stormed toward him. "You orchestrated that death-bed promise?"

"Of course. And I did it for your own good. If you'd gotten together and had a child, it would have become Dr. Benjamin's medical experiment. He would have used your child to plan a phrase three and four and so on and so on. It wouldn't have stopped, and it had to stop. Can't you see how much misery the Cyrene Project has caused? Natalie, your parents were miserable. Rick's, too."

"That didn't mean Natalie and I would have the same fate," Rick pointed out. "Yet, you decided to play God, just like Dr. Benjamin. Now, tell me, how does that make you any different from him?"

"I have your best interests at heart. He doesn't. He merely sees you as his own personal science experiments." Carlton cursed under his breath. "And now, he's got his wish. That baby growing inside you is the abomination that he's worked thirty years to achieve."

Rick hadn't thought his anger could reach any higher, but he was wrong. Natalie caught onto his arm, probably because she feared he was about to launch himself at his uncle.

And he was.

"Carlton, it's time for you to leave," Natalie instructed.

"I will, but my warning still stands. Don't get involved with Rick. If you do, Dr. Benjamin wins."

"This is about winning?" Rick snapped. He eased Natalie aside so he could face his uncle.

"Not just about winning. But about letting a man like Benjamin have his way. He thinks he can run over people, and he can't. Show him that he can't."

"At the moment, how I feel about Dr. Benjamin is a lot more charitable than how I feel about you," Rick informed him. "Natalie was right. It's time for you to go."

Carlton opened his mouth as if to say something, but then he stopped and shook his head. He hurried out the door.

Rick took a moment to get his teeth unclenched so he could speak. "I need you to ask Kitt for the number of the PI she hired."

"Why?" Natalie asked. She studied his face, probably trying to make sure that he was all right. He was. For the most part. But it might take him a lifetime to get over the anger he felt for what Carlton had done. It was a betrayal of the worst sort. Because he'd loved and trusted the man.

"Because I want someone to follow Carlton."

She continued to study him. "You think that's necessary?"

"Unfortunately, yes."

Natalie didn't disagree. Which meant she'd come to the same conclusion.

Carlton couldn't be trusted.

Rick cursed softly. How could he have been so

wrong about his own uncle? Better yet—why had Carlton felt it his duty to become his protector?

Natalie went upstairs to get the number from Kitt, and Rick checked the front drive to make sure their trio of guests had actually left the premises. They had. The only vehicle parked in front was Natalie's car.

Rick went to the bar and poured himself a single shot of whiskey. He took it in one gulp. It didn't help clear his head as he'd hoped it would do, but then that was asking a lot of even good whiskey. Natalie and he had just been delivered yet another blow, and they'd learned that a death-bed promise they'd made was basically a sham. Orchestrated by the one person that he thought was on his side.

No amount of whiskey was going to make that easier to accept.

Natalie came into the room and immediately noted the empty shot glass. "Are you okay?"

"Sure," he lied. "You?"

"Just fine."

The corner of his mouth lifted so he could let her know that her lie wasn't very good.

"We'll get through this," she added, and she handed him a yellow sticky note. "That's the number for the PI, but Kitt's calling him now. She said she'll instruct him to put a tail on Carlton."

Good. Because Rick didn't want his uncle within fifty miles of Natalie. Even if Carlton wasn't the

person trying to kill them, Rick didn't want Natalie
or his child exposed to that kind of bigotry and
warped thinking.

Rick slipped the number into his pocket. "Does
Kitt need us to stay here tonight?"

Natalie shook her head. "No. In fact, she thinks
it'll be best if we go back to my house. The doctor's
on the way, and Kitt's going to ask that Macy be
given a mild sedative to help her sleep."

At least someone would be sleeping tonight, but
Rick didn't think that would extend to him. His mind
was racing with everything he'd learned and with
how he was going to come to terms with it.

He slipped his arm around Natalie's waist to get
her moving toward the door. With luck, he'd be able
to get her to rest. With luck. Of course, Natalie had
the same issues to deal with as he did.

They made their way out the door and down the
steps. Rick heard the sound.

A snap.

He saw the shadowy figure step out from the side
of the house, and Rick automatically pushed Natalie
behind him.

"What—" But she didn't finish. Probably because
it wasn't necessary. She followed his gaze and saw
what had prompted his response.

It was Troy.

"I've been waiting to talk to you," Troy greeted.
He stayed in the shadows, but Rick didn't need to see

his face to know that the man was furious. Rick could hear that fury in his voice.

"Go back inside," Rick told Natalie.

She didn't. Not right away. Because her arm was touching his, he felt her muscle tense. He also felt the argument she was having with herself. She didn't want to leave him alone to face this irate man, but she also couldn't put the baby at risk.

"I need to talk to Natalie, too," Troy insisted.

"Tough. Whatever you have to say to her, you can say to me." Rick didn't take his eyes off Troy, and he gave Natalie a nudge to get her moving. She hurried up the steps and opened the door. What she didn't do was go inside. She stood in the doorway, watching them.

Well, she watched for a few seconds, and then she shouted. "Kitt, call the police. Troy's here."

That brought Troy out of the shadows. With a feral-sounding snarl, he charged right at Rick. Rick was ready for him, too. When Troy got closer, Rick aimed his fist at the man's jaw. And connected.

Hard.

Troy's head jerked back and he staggered, trying to maintain his balance. He also tried to punch Rick. But Rick merely dodged the attempted blow and landed another punch in the guy's solar plexus.

Troy went down like a bag of rocks.

So much for his beefcake body and his superior DNA. It hadn't helped him one iota in a physical confrontation. Of course, Rick had been a lot more motivated than Troy. Rick had been protecting Natalie and his baby.

Natalie rushed down the steps. She had a large umbrella in her hand, and she aimed it at Troy. With that fierce look on her face, Rick didn't doubt she was ready and willing to use it. But it wasn't necessary. Troy stayed on the steps, groaning in pain.

"The cops are on the way," Kitt relayed from the doorway. "Do you need something to tie him up?"

Rick shook his head. "I don't think he's going anywhere."

But Troy tried to prove him wrong. He rolled to his side, looked up at Rick and made eye contact.

"This isn't over," Troy warned. "You had me fired. You turned Macy against me, and you ruined my life. One way or the other, you'll pay me back for that."

"Is that a threat?" Natalie asked.

"You bet it is."

And then Troy made one more huge mistake. He got up. Not empty-handed, either. He pulled a snub-nosed revolver from his pocket.

Adrenaline and panic sliced through Rick.

He dove toward Natalie, to drag her out of harm's way, but he soon realized it wasn't necessary.

Troy turned and broke into a run.

Chapter Fourteen

Natalie dabbed some hydrogen peroxide on Rick's scraped knuckles. She blew on them to take away the sting and then added a kiss for good measure.

"Feel better?" Natalie asked.

"No." But then, his puzzled look over that hand kiss turned into a smile. "Well, a little."

She stared down at him where he was sitting on the edge of her marble bathtub. "Well, I certainly feel better."

"You didn't mind me pulverizing Troy?"

"No." She recapped the peroxide and put it back in the medicine cabinet. "I only wish I had the physical strength to do it myself. Troy deserved what you did to him."

It hadn't taken Rick long to catch up with the man and wrestle him to the ground—where he kept Troy pinned until the police arrived. Sometime within the next twenty-four hours, her mother's former assistant would be booked on attempted assault and carrying a concealed weapon without a permit. None of those charges would land him much jail time, but Natalie prayed it would scare him enough to stay away from Rick and her.

Rick obviously didn't believe that.

After they'd arrived back at her house, Rick had gone on another security tirade, rushing through the rooms while he checked all the windows and the doors. It'd taken her nearly a half hour to lure him into her bathroom so she could disinfect the scrapes on his knuckles that he'd gotten in the altercation with Troy.

"I never thought Carlton would do something like this," he mumbled.

Natalie slid her hand onto his shoulder. "Neither did I." And that was an understatement. She hadn't believed anyone would do something like this. "He manipulated a dying man to keep us apart. It doesn't lessen the pain of David's death, but it does ease the guilt."

"Does it?" he asked.

She nodded. "I have to believe it does. David wasn't well. I know that now, and he was easily manipulated. Heck, I manipulated him. He knew I wasn't in love with him, that I would never be in love with him, yet he asked me to marry him."

"You didn't manipulate that."

"I did by saying yes. If I'd declined, then maybe David would be alive today."

"And maybe David would have killed himself sooner," Rick pointed out. "As you said, he wasn't well."

Natalie leaned against the sink. "Still, we have to live with what happened."

"And we have to live with what Carlton did," Rick added.

Yes, that too.

Natalie knew which would be harder. "Eventually, I'll be able to forgive your uncle. With time. But I don't think I'll ever be able to forgive myself."

He looked up at her. "Let's go back to that night. If David hadn't been a part of the picture, what would you have done when I kissed you?"

"Is that a trick question?" Because she was certain he knew the answer.

"No. What would you have done?"

"Exactly what I did—I kissed you back." She paused, thought about it a moment. Images started to flood her mind. "The kissing would have escalated. At some point, we would have probably decided it was stupid to resist each other because of our over-bearing parents."

"And?" There was some heat in his voice now.

Natalie felt that heat drift her way. "And we would have kept kissing until we dragged each other off to the linen closet."

The corner of his mouth lifted. "The linen closet?"

"It was the nearest place. Since this is my fantasy

account of what might have happened, I get to choose the location."

Without breaking the eye contact between them, he slid his arm around her waist and pulled her to him. "So, let's rewrite history."

Without waiting for her to agree, Rick kissed her.

Natalie hadn't had time to brace herself for the onslaught, and as a result, she lost her breath almost immediately. She didn't care. Breathing didn't seem nearly as important as what Rick was doing with his mouth.

Oh. He was good.

But Natalie had never doubted that.

He looked good, but tasted even better. He touched the seam of her mouth with his tongue. A warning, of sorts, that he was about to deepen the kiss.

He did.

And Natalie felt herself melt against him.

"There's no linen closet in here," she said against his mouth.

"We don't need one. We've got everything we need right here."

And he proceeded to prove that to her.

RICK SNAPPED Natalie to him and pulled her onto his lap. He took her mouth, feasting on it.

"The no-kissing rule obviously is out the window," she remarked.

"Yeah. It went out with that no-sex rule."

"Good."

That was it. The only green light he needed from Natalie. They were finally going to have sex, and this time he'd make sure they both remembered it.

Natalie obviously agreed because she wound her arms around him, readjusted herself, and moved her legs to either side of his hips. Straddling him. All in all, it was a darn good position—except, of course, they were in the bathroom. Her big, comfortable bed was only yards away, but judging from the heat of their kisses, that bed was a million miles away.

Without breaking the kiss or the body contact, Rick eased them to the floor, and he somehow managed to do that with Natalie still in his lap. The new position must have created a new urgency in her because she went after his T-shirt. It was a frenzied motion, and for some reason speed seemed to count here.

Rick didn't like speed when it came to sex.

So, he helped her with his T-shirt removal and then caught onto her hands. When he took her mouth again, he did so slowly, hoping it would set the pace.

It didn't.

Natalie obviously didn't like slow when it came to sex.

She pressed herself closer and closer until it was hard to tell where he started and she began. When she slid her hand between their bodies and went after his zipper, Rick remembered which parts were his and which were hers.

Rick tried a different tactic and eased her back onto the thick white rug that covered the floor. He followed on top of her. A temporary move. Just so he could get control of her clever, zipper-lowering hands.

"Oh, this is good," she mumbled. And to prove her point, she made some adjustments of her own and cradled his hips with her thighs. She also nudged him with the center of her body and had him seeing stars.

Oh, man.

This was not going to be a long session of love-making if she kept doing that.

"Plan B," he whispered. "I take you here, now, and later we do this the right way."

"We're doing it the right way," she insisted. "I like having your weight on me."

Okay. He'd remember that. Since he liked having her beneath him, this was working out pretty good. Of course, he would have equally enjoyed having her on top.

Heck, he just wanted her.

Everything else was optional.

Since she was going on another zipper-finding mission, Rick made a counterstrike. He went after her zipper. Well, her panties anyway. He slid his hand up her dress and found a little swatch of silk and lace. Despite Natalie's nudges and mumbled pleas for more, he took a moment to savor her choice of underwear. He circled his fingers over the fabric, making sure he also circled his fingers over her.

She moaned softly and lifted her hips.

He liked that reaction very much so he upped the stakes. He rid Natalie of those panties and touched her with his fingers. She was wet and hot. Oh, and she was ready.

He tossed the panties aside, and with some maneuvering, he slid down her body. And replaced his fingers with his mouth.

She said something very, very dirty.

That caused him to smile, but he stayed focused on the pleasurable task at hand. He sampled. Savored. Enjoyed. And judging from the names she was calling him, Natalie was enjoying it, too.

Well, for a few moments anyway.

She caught onto him and forced him to make his way back up her body. Rick dropped a few kisses on her stomach along the way.

"I want you in me," she said.

And it was a powerful demand. Especially coupled with the fact that she was stripping off the rest of his clothes. Rick decided to strip off her clothes as well.

Her bra distracted him a moment. He was a sucker for white lace, and that's what she had on beneath that little peach dress. Despite her insistence that they get on with this, he kissed her nipples through the lace. It was definitely an erogenous zone for her because she slid her fingers into his hair and pulled him closer.

Man, it was exciting to learn what excited her.

Rick continued to excite them both a little longer, but Natalie soon began tugging and pulling him until she had him between her legs.

"Now," she demanded.

He gave her *now*.

Rick watched her as he took her. Her eyelids fluttered down. Her mouth opened slightly. Her breath deepened.

Inch by inch he entered her. The sensations were overwhelming. The pleasure. The feel of being inside her. The way she moved against him. And then, with him.

The rhythm they found was as old as time itself. Easy and slow. Then, building. Escalating. To a frantic pace. Until it was unbearable.

His body begged for release. So did Natalie's. He could feel her so close to that release. He could see it on her face. So he pushed into her.

She met his gaze at the exact moment he felt her surrender. Rick moved deep inside her, giving and capturing as much of the pleasure as he could.

Then he kissed her.

One hot kiss.

And the taste of her was all he needed to send him over the edge. Rick buried his face against hers and let go.

RICK HEARD the peaceful rhythm of Natalie's breathing. She'd fallen asleep once he moved her into the bedroom. Thank God. She'd been exhausted and hadn't been getting nearly enough peace and quiet.

Well, it felt peaceful and quiet now.

It also felt right.

He frowned at that *right* feeling and reminded himself that just because they no longer were bound by that promise they'd made to David, it didn't mean they were a couple.

Yes, they'd had sex, but it was just that. Sex. Between two people who'd always been attracted to each other. Sex was a natural progression—which seemed ironic since Natalie was already pregnant with his baby.

That whole natural progression had obviously skipped a few steps, thanks to whoever had drugged them.

But where would the steps take them now?

Rick didn't have a lot of time to contemplate that because his cell phone rang. Natalie woke up. Of course. And he rifled through his clothes to locate the phone so he could chew out the person who'd called and disturbed her much-needed sleep.

"It's me, Carlton."

Oh, man. Rick definitely wasn't ready for round two with his uncle. "We have nothing more to say to each other."

"But we do. Don't hang up. Please."

It was the *please* that caught his attention. "I'm listening," Rick finally said. "But make it quick."

"Okay. Here goes. I've been investigating what happened to Natalie and you, and I tracked down the missing bartender, Brandon Stevens."

"Where is he?"

"At this exact moment, I don't know, but he's agreed to meet us at a bar down on the Riverwalk. He's scared, Rick. He says someone tried to run him off the road. And get this—it was an SUV with dark tinted windows."

Well, that was a puzzle piece that actually fitted—if the bartender was telling the truth, that is. "Is he willing to come to Natalie's house? I can meet him outside."

With Natalie tucked *inside.* Where she'd be safe.

"He says he'll only meet us at the well-lit area in front of the Yellow Rose Bar," Carlton explained. "It's open all night. He says that's the only place he'll feel safe since he knows the area well and there'll be people around."

Safety was a big issue for Rick, too, and this didn't sound safe. "Then, have him call me so we can talk."

"He wants to talk to you in person," Carlton said without hesitation.

His uncle's lack of hesitation, however, caused Rick's uneasiness to rise. "Why?"

"I don't know. Like I said—he's scared."

But fear could be faked, and even if it was real, it didn't mean this meeting was a good idea. "Is this some kind of trap?" Rick asked point-blank.

"No. Not by me, it's not. But I can't vouch for the bartender's motives. That's why I'm meeting you there. I'll be your back-up."

"I don't trust you to be my back-up." Rick didn't even have to think about this.

"I know. And I'm sorry about that. Hell, I'm sorry about everything I said and everything I did. I can't make that up to you. I know it. But I can stop someone from trying to hurt Natalie and you. This Brandon Stevens seems to know who's responsible for that. He even says he has proof."

Rick met Natalie's gaze. He could see the conflict going on in her eyes. Proof was something they were sorely lacking. Was it possible this bartender had that kind of proof? And could this proof lead to the arrest of a would-be killer?

He didn't have to debate it long. Rick knew this was a meeting he'd have to attend, even if such a meeting was setting off all kinds of alarms in his head.

"Give me an hour," Rick told his uncle. "I need to make some arrangements before I can leave."

"Sure. And, Rick, be careful. Bring your gun."

Oh, he intended to do just that.

But even with precautions, Rick figured this could be a deadly meeting.

Chapter Fifteen

"You know you're not coming with me to the bar, right?" Rick asked as he strapped on a shoulder holster and slipped his gun inside it.

She knew she was staying home. Natalie had figured that out as soon as she'd heard Rick agree to the meeting. He would have never agreed to it if it meant taking her with him. The risk to the baby was just too high.

But so was the risk for Rick.

"I don't want you to go," she said, knowing she couldn't change his mind.

"I don't want to go, either, but we have to put a stop to this. We can't keep looking over our shoulders, waiting for someone to make the next attempt on our lives."

He was right. There would be another attempt. And probably the attempts would continue until this person got what they wanted—the two of them dead.

But was Carlton the very person responsible?

"The PI is on his way over," Rick explained. "Kitt trusts him. She says he'll protect you if necessary."

Natalie didn't doubt it. Her sister's recommendation was enough to know she'd be in good hands. "And who'll protect you?" she asked Rick.

He shrugged. "I can take care of myself."

She caught onto his arm and turned him around to face her. "Swear to me that's true."

Rick touched his mouth to hers. "I swear."

He didn't add more, probably because at that exact moment the doorbell rang. Rick maneuvered her into the living room and hurried to answer it.

But not before drawing his weapon.

Natalie peeked out, hating that she couldn't be standing side by side with him in case there was danger waiting behind that door. She hated that she couldn't help him. But the pregnancy changed everything.

She let out the breath she'd been holding when Rick opened the door and let the tall, wide-shouldered man inside. They made introductions. He was Mason Tanner, and judging from his brawny build and seemingly permanent scowl, he was formidable. No wonder her sister had hired him.

"Stay put," Rick told her. "I'll call you as soon as I know something."

She nodded. "You'll be careful." And she refused to make it sound like a question. It couldn't be a question. He had to come back to her.

"Absolutely." He kissed her and ran his hand lovingly over her stomach. "Stay safe."

"You do the same."

That was it. The only goodbye that time allowed. As it was, Rick would have to hurry to make it to the meeting in time. He glanced over his shoulder and winked at her as he headed out the door.

That wink was playful and sexy enough, but it didn't make Natalie feel better about what he was doing. Nothing would at this point. Well, nothing except having Rick safely back in her arms.

While the PI rearmed the security system and locked the door, Natalie went to the window to watch Rick ride away on his motorcycle, headed toward God-knows-what fate.

RICK SLIPPED his hand inside his leather jacket and gripped his gun. The Yellow Rose Bar was too public and too crowded for him to go inside with his weapon drawn. But he wanted to have it handy just in case.

He only hoped *just in case* wouldn't become necessary.

"I'm over here," he heard Carlton say.

Rick automatically tensed, and his fingers tightened around the gun. He spotted his uncle outside the bar, standing beneath a perky awning painted with huge yellow roses.

"You can trust me," Carlton added, obviously sensing that Rick wasn't at ease.

"Trust isn't the issue here. Let's get this finished. Where's Brandon Stevens?"

Carlton shook his head. "He's hasn't shown up yet."

Hell. Rick hoped this wasn't a wild-goose chase.

"How's Natalie?" Carlton asked.

"Let's not do small talk."

"It wasn't. I genuinely want to know."

Rick was still skeptical, but he answered anyway. "She's scared and too stubborn to admit she's scared. And I'm scared for her and the baby."

Carlton nodded. "The bartender will tell us what we need to know. He wants the person responsible to be arrested so he can clear his own name. He's afraid if he doesn't do that, then the cops will eventually try to pin all of this on him."

He just stared at his uncle. "Is this an act?"

"No."

Rick made a sound to indicate he wasn't sure he believed Carlton, and he scanned the area to see if their informant was going to show. There were plenty of twenty-something guys hanging around, but none of them appeared to be there for a critical meeting.

His uncle's phone rang, and he reached into his pocket to retrieve it. That's when he noticed that Carlton was armed as well.

"It's the bartender," Carlton said, passing his phone to Rick. "He wants to talk to you."

Rick cursed. He hadn't come all this way for a

phone call. He wanted to meet the man face to face. "Where are you?" Rick demanded.

"Nearby. I can see you, but I'm not sure it's safe for me to be there with you."

Rick glanced around, at the Riverwalk itself and then at the buildings that lined both sides of the narrow river.

"It's as safe for you as it is for me," Rick pointed out. And because he suddenly felt very threatened, he kept an eye on Carlton. He didn't want to be ambushed.

"I think I have something that can help us both with our safety issues," Brandon continued. "I know who drugged you. If I give you this person's name, swear to me that you'll do everything within your power to stop what's happening."

It sounded sort of reasonable, except for one glaring thing. "Why didn't you just go to the police with this?"

"Because I can't. There's a warrant out there for my arrest. A hit and run. It has nothing to do with what happened to you."

Rick decided to withhold judgment on that. "So, who drugged me at Ms. Sinclair's party?"

"Dr. Claude Benjamin."

Since Benjamin was one of their prime suspects, Rick wasn't surprised. "What kind of proof do you have?"

"My word."

"Oh, and with that arrest warrant hanging over your head, your word's not worth much, is it?"

"It'll have to do because I don't think the doctor wants either of us to live. We're witnesses to his crime, and I think he'd rather see us both dead."

"How did Benjamin do it?" Rick asked. "How did he drug Natalie Sinclair and me?"

"He came in through the kitchen while the party was going on, and he gave me a beer. He described you and said I was to give it to you."

That was possible. "What about Natalie?"

"The same. He put something in her drink as well and told me to take it to her. He said I didn't have to worry about the security cameras filming me because he would jam the equipment at various times through the evening."

Well, that explained that, but it didn't explain something that was causing Rick's blood pressure to rise. "And at no point did you think about stopping yourself from participating in a felony?"

"Of course I thought about it. But this doctor knew about my problems with the law, and he said he'd call the police if I didn't do as I was told."

And Benjamin no doubt had used that as leverage to get the guy to cooperate.

"Why didn't the doctor just bring the drinks to us himself?"

"He said he wasn't supposed to be there at the estate, that he'd had a big disagreement with Natalie's mother and that she would have him thrown out if she spotted him."

That was probably true, but it also made Rick wonder—had Dr. Benjamin been drugging Macy as well? Someone certainly had and he was the most likely candidate. But why had he drugged her? Maybe to gain her cooperation?

"I need proof," Rick insisted. "I can't go to the police with just hearsay."

"I know, and I'm willing to come in and testify, if you can get the police to drop the other charges."

"You swear to that?"

"Absolutely. I don't want Dr. Benjamin out on the streets any more than you."

Rick had no idea how he was going to convince the police to bargain, but he had to try. Maybe he could even get the feds involved so they could offer Brandon Stevens protective custody and immunity until they'd built their case against Benjamin and the Cyrene Project.

"I'll go to the police first thing in the morning," Rick promised the man. "Give me a number where I can reach you."

Brandon hesitated, but he finally provided a cell phone number. Rick scribbled it down on the palm of his hand, ended the call and handed Carlton back his cell phone.

"If you need anything, just let me know," Carlton called out as Rick headed back to his motorcycle.

Rick didn't acknowledge the offer. Instead, he took out his own phone so he could call Natalie. She was no doubt on pins and needles waiting to hear from him. The problem was—he didn't know if what he'd learned would truly help them. If Brandon was telling the truth, he had the name of the person responsible for drugging them.

Now, the question was—how was he going to get the police to arrest a prominent doctor solely on the word of a man with an outstanding arrest warrant?

Hell.

With that reminder, Rick decided to skip the call to Natalie. First, he'd go to police headquarters and give them the information about Dr. Benjamin. With luck, the doctor would be behind bars before morning. Then, he'd finally have some good news to pass on to Natalie.

"Don't answer the phone," the PI, Mason Tanner, warned Natalie.

She stopped in mid-step. Or rather she stopped in mid-run, because she was practically sprinting across the room to get to the phone. It was probably Rick with an update of how the meeting went.

And she'd finally learn whether he was safe.

"What's wrong?" she asked.

Tanner lifted his left hand in a stay-quiet gesture, and he continued to look out the window. "I'm not sure. But something's not right."

Natalie huffed. "Yes, the phone is ringing, and I'm not answering it."

He didn't respond. He just stood there, his entire body postured for…something.

But what?

"Rick will be worried if I don't answer that," she pointed out.

"Rick will be worried if I don't keep you safe." He took a gun from his shoulder holster. "Step away from the windows. Kill the lights. I think someone might be out there."

Natalie had been more annoyed than alarmed.

Until Mason Tanner said that.

But the stark tone of his voice had her obeying. She stepped back into the corner of the living room, so that she could still keep an eye on Tanner, and she turned off the lights.

He, in turn, kept an eye on whatever he thought might be outside that window, though he did make a quick check of the security panel.

Tanner cursed. "Something's wrong with the security system."

"What?"

"It's not working. The indication lights and motion detectors are all dead." With that horrifying revelation, he lifted his head, listening.

Natalie listened, too, but it was difficult to hear much because her heartbeat was pounding in her ears.

She wished she had a gun, but as far as she knew there wasn't one in the house. So, she made do. She grabbed a fire poker and raised it in front of her in case she had to defend herself.

While she stood there, waiting, bracing herself for the worst, Natalie considered her options.

She could try to call 911, but she'd left her cell phone in the bathroom. The house phone was on the table, on the other side of the room. She considered getting it and trying to call Rick. Or the police. However, that table was directly in front of a window. Where Tanner had warned her not to go. Besides, it probably wasn't even working. If someone had managed to tamper with the security system, then they would have no doubt cut the phone line as well. So, that left her with no immediate way to contact Rick and no defense other than Mason Tanner and a fire poker.

Then, she heard the sound.

Not her heartbeat; it was a swish.

Like someone roughly blowing out a candle.

A second later, she heard another sound. It came from Tanner. A sort of grunt. And she watched in horror as he collapsed onto the floor.

"Oh, God." She started to go to him, but another sound stopped her.

Footsteps.

Natalie followed their sound and quickly spotted the source. There were two men in the sunroom on the other side of the foyer.

Two armed men.

Even in the darkness she could see their weapons.

One of them carried a rifle. One of them had no doubt shot Tanner, probably with a gun rigged with a silencer. That's why there'd only been the swish of sound and not a heavy blast. And it likely meant they'd used the silencer so they wouldn't alert any of her neighbors.

Of course, it also meant they'd probably come there to murder her.

Natalie ducked back into the corner of the room. And she prayed. First, that Tanner was all right. But she also prayed that Rick didn't walk in on this. If he did, those two men would likely kill him on the spot.

She listened to those footsteps. They moved toward Tanner, and she heard the two men mumble something. They didn't fire another shot. They didn't begin an interrogation or toss out any remarks.

Did that mean Tanner was already dead?

Her breath turned heavy and thick, and she fought to keep control so that she wouldn't hyperventilate. It wasn't easy to do with her heart racing out of control and the adrenaline surging through her. This was a fight-or-flight situation, but in a fight with two gunmen, she'd lose.

And so would her unborn baby.

Still, she had to do something. Not just for her sake. But for Tanner's. If by some miracle he was still alive, he would need medical attention.

Natalie knew if she didn't run, Tanner and she would likely die. So, she forced herself to react. To move. Trying to stay as quiet as possible, she side-stepped around the room. Keeping in the shadows. Trying not to panic.

One step at a time, she reminded herself. One step at a time.

If she made it out of there, she could perhaps get to her bathroom upstairs so she could retrieve her cell phone. Or maybe she could go to Kitt's office. It was downstairs, making it more accessible to her, but she had no idea if her sister had a cell phone in there or not.

"One step at a time," she mouthed.

She kept her attention nailed to the foyer. There was movement out there, and whispered voices, but she couldn't see what was happening. Natalie kept moving, and she made it all the way to the arched doorway that led to the back hall.

Just as a bullet slammed into the wall right next to her head.

RICK PARKED his Harley behind Natalie's car and climbed off. He also cursed. He wouldn't be delivering any good news tonight.

The police were checking into Brandon Stevens' allegations. That was it—they were checking into it. They'd given Rick no timeline for it, and they'd also given him no hope that this would lead to Dr. Benjamin's arrest.

Still, he wouldn't give up. He couldn't. There was too much at stake.

He went up the steps and was a little surprised that Natalie or Mason Tanner didn't automatically open the door. He figured the PI would be keeping watch. But he checked the time. It was late. It was possible Natalie had already gone to her room and that the PI was in another part of the house.

Rick reached for the doorbell.

And stopped.

He immediately rethought that part about Natalie having gone to her room. She wouldn't have. She would have been waiting for him to return, and she would have done that downstairs.

So where was she?

He leaned over and peered through the window. Everything seemed okay. Nothing out of place.

Well, nothing except for the fact that the lights were off and there was no sign of Natalie.

Using just the knuckle of his left index finger, he rapped once on the window. It was faint, but it was also a test. To see if it would cause the PI to check it out.

Nothing.

And that *nothing* sent a shot of fear and dread through him. Hell.

Something was wrong.

Rick tested the front door—it was locked. So, while he drew his gun, he leapt from the porch and started to run. He raced around to the back of the house, intending to go in through the sunroom, but along the way, he spotted something he hadn't wanted to see.

An open window to Kitt's office.

Since the floodlights were still working, he could see that the shrubs beneath the window had been trampled and the screen was lying on the ground. Someone had used this window to gain entry to the house.

He made a split-second glance inside to make sure that someone wasn't in the room. Like the foyer, it was empty and dark so Rick climbed inside, waited a couple of seconds for his eyes to adjust to the darkness, and then he began his search for Natalie. She had to be all right.

She just had to be.

Keeping his footsteps as light as possible, he made his way through Kitt's equipment-cluttered office, checking the corners and the shadows to make sure no one was lurking there. He couldn't risk being ambushed. He had to stay alive and well so he could get to Natalie.

When he made it to the hall outside the office, he heard the sound of voices. Not shouts. But a whispered conversation between at least two people.

Two men.

Was one of them Dr. Benjamin?

Had the doctor come to finish what he'd started?

Rick didn't go toward those voices. Instead, he headed in the opposite direction and followed the hall into the kitchen and the adjacent butler's pantry. They were both empty as well.

Where the heck was Natalie?

The question had no sooner formed in his head than he sensed the movement in the room. He froze and listened. Waiting. For whatever, or whomever, he was about to encounter.

There were no more whispered voices, just the faint rush of the A/C and the hum of the refrigerator. But beneath those sounds, he was certain he heard something else.

Someone breathing.

It was strange, but he thought he might recognize that breathing.

"Natalie?" he whispered.

The breathing stopped, and for a few heart-stopping moments, all he heard was silence.

"Rick?"

It was Natalie. He was sure of it.

He spun in the direction of Natalie's voice and spotted her peering out from the doorway of the dining room. Even though the only illumination came from the light over the stove, he could see her. She looked terrified, but she was alive.

Thank God.

She had a fire poker in her right hand, and she put her finger to her lips to indicate that he should stay quiet. He did. But he made his way toward her. He wanted more than anything to take her into his arms. To hold her. To reassure himself that she was real and safe. But even a hug was a luxury they couldn't risk. Obviously, something had gone horribly wrong.

"There are two gunmen in the house," she whispered. "They shot Tanner."

Oh, man. That news hit him hard, mainly because he knew if they'd shot Tanner, then Natalie had likely come close to being shot herself.

"Do you know where they are?" Rick mouthed.

"I think in the front hall."

In other words, too close. But then, just the fact they were in the house meant they were too close.

He caught onto her arm and led her toward the massive pantry just off the kitchen. It wouldn't give them much protection if those gunmen started firing, but it would give him a chance to use his cell phone to call 911.

"Are you okay?" he asked her as he took out his phone. He also kept a firm grip on his gun.

She nodded. "I was scared you'd walk in on this and they'd shoot you."

He mentally groaned. Leave it to Natalie to be more concerned about him than she was herself. But thank God she'd somehow managed to evade those gunmen. Now, it was up to him to continue evading them so Natalie and he could escape. Once he had her out of harm's way, then he could figure out who these SOBs were.

He punched in 911, cringing at the tiny beeps his phone made with each number. He put the phone to his ear—and immediately realized his cell phone had been jammed.

That sent his stomach to his knees. Because he didn't think it was a coincidence. No way. It meant someone had planned this and planned it well. They also had access to some sophisticated jamming equipment.

"We're getting out of here," he let Natalie know.

He only hoped it wasn't too late.

He glanced out the pantry door. The kitchen was still empty. No voices, either. So, he caught onto Natalie's arm to get her moving.

They'd only made it a few steps before someone fired at them.

The silenced shot smacked into the wooden frame of the pantry door.

He lunged to the floor, behind a kitchen island, and dragged Natalie down with him.

But it was too late.

There was a second bullet, and Rick knew what had happened from the sound that Natalie made.

She'd been shot.

Chapter Sixteen

Natalie felt the jolt.

It was followed almost instantly by the fire. Mercy, her right leg burned. And she lost control of her muscles. Because she had no choice, she toppled onto Rick.

"You've been shot," she heard him say. His voice was so frantic that she didn't recognize it at first. It took even longer for her to realize what he'd said.

She'd been shot.

That was the reason her leg was burning. That was the reason for the pain.

She didn't panic, but she had one horrifying thought. If her injury was serious enough, if she lost enough blood, she could lose the baby.

Oh, God.

She could lose the baby.

Natalie choked back a sob. Until now, until this horrible moment, she hadn't realized just how much she loved and wanted this child.

And she hadn't realized just how much she loved and wanted Rick.

She only hoped she got the chance to tell him.

Rick pulled her over to him, pushed her against the kitchen island and sheltered her with his own body. He didn't stop there. While he kept his gun ready, he reached down and clamped his left hand over her leg.

There was blood.

Lots of it.

Natalie could feel herself going into shock, but she fought it hard. She couldn't lose control. She couldn't lose consciousness. She had to help Rick if they had any hopes of staying alive.

She dropped the fire poker, moved his hand aside and formed her own compress, pressing her fingers against the wound to slow the bleeding. Rick took advantage of his free hand. He lifted his head, took aim and fired.

One of the men howled in pain, and she heard him crash to the floor.

"Good," Natalie snarled.

She wanted both gunmen dead or at least out of commission so they could call an ambulance for Tanner and her. Then the police could figure out who had hired these goons to come after them.

Natalie reached up into the drawer and grabbed a dishtowel. While she tried to keep a vigilant watch to make sure that the second gunman didn't circle around and shoot them, she made a makeshift tourniquet.

Rick was vigilant as well, and he eased out a few inches from the island, probably so he could keep better surveillance of the room.

It also put him in more danger.

Natalie was about to pull him back toward her when there was a shot. It slammed into the kitchen island and was quickly followed by another bullet.

And another.

Who was doing this?

And why did they want to kill Rick and her?

The shots splintered the cabinets and the tile countertop and sent a dangerous spray of debris raining over them. She ducked down and sheltered her eyes.

Rick didn't though.

Much to her horror, he reared up and fired.

He ducked back down just as there was another round of gunfire.

All aimed at him.

Six shots. Natalie counted them, even though she had no idea how many bullets their assailant's firearm could hold. Worse, the remaining gunman probably didn't have just one weapon. After all, she'd seen that rifle.

The shots stopped.

And Natalie began to fumble around for the fire poker that she'd dropped moments earlier. It wasn't much of a weapon, but it was better than nothing.

"Enough of this," the gunman snarled. And he said something else that Natalie couldn't distinguish.

Then, she heard the other voice.

There was another person in the room.

God, was it a third gunman?

Natalie glanced at Rick and met his gaze briefly. "I'll get you out of this. I swear."

She knew he meant it, but she also knew this might be out of his control. There might be no human way for him to keep them alive.

"Natalie? Rick?" someone called out. "Let's end this game now."

Natalie instantly recognized that voice.

"What do you want?" Rick demanded, apparently recognizing it as well.

"Simple," Dr. Isabella Henderson calmly said. "I'm here to kill you."

RICK DIDN'T HAVE to ask her motive. He knew. Dr. Benjamin had already spelled it out. Isabella Henderson was a woman with a sterling career ahead of her, and her involvement with the Cyrene Project could cost her everything.

And it could send her to jail.

Rick intended that to happen, one way or another.

"You honestly think I'm just going to let you try to kill us?" Rick asked the doctor.

"I don't think you have a choice. I'm well-armed, and so is my *assistant*. You, on the other hand, have only one weapon, and Natalie is bleeding out. We can just stand here and wait for her to die."

That put a hard knot in Rick's gut. "Or?" He waited for the compromise he hoped the doctor would offer. Maybe she would let him trade his life for Natalie's.

"There is no *or*," she explained. "I don't intend to let either of you walk out of here. In fact, if you'd been here when we arrived like I'd thought you would be, I'd planned a quick shoot-and-kill through the windows. You never would have seen it coming. There can be no proof of the Cyrene Project, and as long as you're alive, you, Natalie, and especially your baby are the ultimate proof."

Hell. Rick was afraid that's where this conversation was going. "What do you intend to do—kill everyone associated with the Cyrene Project?"

"Absolutely. Dr. Benjamin has already left the country. As long as he stays away and remains quiet, he won't be a threat to me. But anyone who knows about my involvement dies. I've already taken care of Troy. That leaves you, Natalie and her sister. Her brother doesn't know about the project, so his life will be spared. Once all the rest of you are dead, then everything is in place to make it look as if drug-crazed Macy killed you. Then, I'm free to pursue my new career objectives in Europe."

There was absolute confidence in the doctor's voice. But Rick was equally confident that he would get Natalie and his baby out of this alive. He glanced at Natalie to reassure her of that, but instead he saw the blood that was spreading across the terrycloth tourniquet. Whatever he was going to do, he had to do it fast. He couldn't risk Natalie losing any more blood.

"I can help you," Natalie mouthed. Her mouth tightened, probably from the pain. "Just tell me what you need me to do, and I'll do it."

He was about to tell Natalie to stay low, where the kitchen island would protect her, but he knew wood and tile would be little protection from bullets. Once the doctor and her hired gun started shooting, and they would, they wouldn't stop until they'd succeeded.

That meant Rick had to take them out first.

"Create a distraction," he whispered to Natalie. "But keep it safe. No unnecessary chances."

She waited a moment, obviously processing his plan, but he could also see that her injury was dazing her. He prayed she wasn't about to lose consciousness. She finally nodded and grabbed his cell phone. While keeping a firm grip on the fire poker, she hurled the phone behind them, into the air. In the direction of their attackers.

Either the doctor or the other man fired.

Natalie didn't stop there. She snatched objects from the drawer where she'd taken the dishcloth. She tossed napkin rings and an oven mitt. Each item garnered a shot and some vicious profanity from the gunman.

That was Rick's cue to do what he had to do. He mentally counted to three and rolled to the side. Out in the open. So he could get a clear shot of at least one of them.

It worked.

A little too well.

Because both the doctor and the gunman took direct aim at him.

He fired, taking out the gunman, and in that instant he knew he wouldn't be able to re-aim and stop the doctor before she stopped him.

There was a split second where he figured he was about to die. Natalie flashed through his mind. So did their baby. A child he loved but might never get to see.

He saw Natalie move out of the corner of his eye, and he shouted for her to get back. It was too late. Dr. Henderson's attention and aim were focused on him so she didn't see the fire poker that Natalie launched at her.

The metal spear collided with the doctor's arm and threw off her aim. For only a moment. But a moment was enough. Rick lifted his weapon and fired.

His shot went into the doctor's chest.

He saw her face. Saw the surprise register before she dropped to the floor. She landed beside the other gunman.

Rick scrambled across the room to retrieve the weapons, just in case. But there was no reason for just in case. He checked for pulses, and both were dead.

He didn't take any time to ponder what had just happened. He only had one thought—get to Natalie.

He raced back across the room, scooped her up into his arms and hurried outside so he could get her to the hospital. And he began to bargain and pray with the powers that be that Natalie and their baby would be all right.

Chapter Seventeen

Natalie considered protesting. For a moment or two she considered telling Rick that she could walk on her own two feet.

Or rather limp on her own two feet.

However, she shut up and let him do what he wanted. And what he wanted was to carry her inside her house.

He eased her from the car, cradling her against him and went up the steps. Yes, it was silly, but there was something hot about Rick carrying her. And no, it wasn't the whole threshold thing. It was the closeness. The intimacy…

Oh, and the fact that it felt so darn good to be in his arms.

"Did I hurt you?" he asked.

Natalie pulled herself from her arm fantasy and tried to figure out what had prompted that. "You're breathing fast," he pointed out.

"Ah. That. No, I'm not in pain."

"Because if you are, the doctor gave you a prescription for some pain meds."

"I'm fine. Really," she added when he stared down at her with a skeptical look.

"You're not fine. You just spent two days in the hospital because that witch, Isabella Henderson, shot you in the leg."

"Yes, but it wasn't a serious wound, and I'm all better. Promise." And because he looked like he needed it, she brushed a kiss on his mouth.

"If that kiss was meant to calm me down, it won't work."

Probably not. Rick had been on somewhat of a rampage since the shooting. He was blaming himself, of course. "Then, maybe this kiss will work."

She tried again. This time, it was long and French.

When she pulled back, she noted that his expression was slightly softer. Slightly.

"You saved my life," she reminded him. "You saved our baby's life."

"I let you get shot."

"No. You did everything in your power to stop it from happening. Big difference."

He eased her into a chair in her sitting room and probably would have moved away from her if Natalie hadn't caught onto his arm.

"Let's do an inventory here," she began. "The PI, Mason Tanner, is critical but stable. He'll recover. That's good. It's also good that the police learned that it was Isabella who jammed your cell phone. So, that means there aren't any accomplices lurking around out there. And some final good news—Dr. Benjamin is behind bars for drugging us and for stealing your lab results so the police wouldn't have any proof that we'd been drugged."

"You're trying to cheer me up."

She nodded. "Is it working?" Because she was afraid he'd say no, she kissed him again. And because she really wanted that dour look gone from his handsome face, she pulled him in to the chair next to her and snuggled against him.

"Yeah," he finally admitted. "It's working."

Natalie smiled. Nudged him with her elbow. And watched him briefly return the smile.

"Carlton sent those." He pointed to a rather large arrangement of yellow roses. Her favorite. The bouquet was beside the three others that Rick had sent her.

"I know it won't happen right away, but one day you might be able to forgive Carlton." Natalie waited to see how he would respond to that.

"Maybe."

Well, that was a lot better than his previous reaction which had had a hell-no ring to it.

Actually, a lot of things had the potential to get better. Now that they knew the truth. That Dr. Henderson and her hired guns had been the only people out to kill them. Not Dr. Benjamin. Not Carlton. Not the bartender. Not even Troy. Natalie had feared that Troy had been working for Dr. Henderson or even Dr. Benjamin, but as the police had discovered, the young man was angry over being fired and angrier still about the Cyrene Project, but he had no real intentions of carrying out his threat to kill them.

"Why have you been able to put all of this behind you?" he asked.

"I haven't. I'll always remember what happened. I'll always remember how close I came to losing you and the baby."

His mouth tightened again. "You could have died."

"*You* could have died," Natalie countered. "And in those moments when the witch was shooting at us, I realized how important you are to me."

The tightness eased a bit. So did the expression in his eyes. "You're important to me, too."

"Whew. For a while there, I thought this was going to be a one-sided confession of my feelings." She paused to gather her thoughts and catch her breath. That stay in the hospital had given her lots of time to think, and she wasn't going to leave it unsaid. "We have a chance to rewrite history, Rick."

Rick probably had an opinion or comment about that, but he didn't get to voice it. Because the stupid phone rang. She groaned at the interruption and answered it with intentions of making it the shortest call in history.

"Hello," Natalie snarled, making sure it didn't sound friendly.

"It's me—Kitt," her sister said with some hesitation. "I just wanted to let you know that I'm getting Mom settled into a nursing home. The place is like a five-star resort—she'll even have room service. And the doctors say she won't be here long. They're expecting a full recovery. But judging from your hello, I'm guessing that you don't want to talk. Still, take the time to answer one quick question—are you all right?"

"I'm fine. And I really, really mean that. Rick is here," Natalie added.

"Oh." Kitt made a naughty sound of approval. "Does that mean it's a bad time for me to have a long, sisterly marathon conversation?"

Natalie didn't even have to think about it. "Yes. It's a bad time for that."

"But you're wounded. You couldn't possibly want to do anything down and dirty with Rick."

"Don't bet on it. Goodbye, Kitt. I'll call you later." She put the phone on the table and turned to Rick.

He met her with a kiss.

A deep, hot kiss.

"Marry me," he said.

Her throat snapped shut, and the blood rushed to her head. "Wh-what?"

She'd expected more sex. Definitely more sex. She even hoped for a few dates so they could settle more comfortably into shared parenthood.

But marriage?

Okay, she hadn't expected it, but she'd thought about it. Too much. In fact, she'd had girlie daydreams about it while in the hospital. A fairy-tale wedding complete with a white dress and all the trimmings.

But there was a problem with those particular daydreams.

"Are you asking me because I'm pregnant?" she wanted to know.

"I'm asking because I want to be your husband."

Natalie let her heart flutter a bit before she shook her head. "Why?"

He ran his hand over her stomach. "We have a chance to rewrite history," he said using her own words. "We can do this, Natalie. You, me, and our own little Harley."

That caused a different kind of flutter. Not a good one, either. "Harley?"

"Not meant to be taken literally, though it would be a suitable name for a boy or a girl. Picture it—a Harley-riding PhD. Beauty and brains. Or for a boy—brawn and brains."

Well, that wasn't a bad thing to picture at all. Natalie smiled, but it quickly faded. "Rick, we can have, uh, Harley and not be married."

He pushed up her dress. Kissed her bandage. And then kissed her bare stomach.

Natalie knew that was meant to be a gentle gesture, but his warm, gusting breath gave her other ideas. Ideas she put on hold. First things first. There was a marriage proposal on the table.

"It's a pity proposal," she informed him.

"You think so?" He began to toy with the elastic on her panties. "Well, it wasn't. I don't do pity orgasms, pity kisses or pity proposals."

"Then, what kind of proposal was it?" she asked.

He toyed some more with her panties and let his breath brush right against the V-junction of her thighs.

"You're trying to distract me," she challenged.

"Yes," he readily admitted. "Because I want you to agree to marry me, and if necessary, I'll get you to say yes while in the throes of oral sex. And before you suggest old-fashioned sex—don't. You're in no shape for that. Yet. Next week, maybe."

Natalie was about to tell him that he was distracting her again, but Rick pulled the ultimate distraction.

"I love you," he said. "That's why I want to marry you. Little Harley is just a bonus. A great bonus. But a bonus nonetheless. You're the prize, Natalie. You're the one I want to grow old with. You're the one I want to have sex with, next week."

And because he was obviously serious about her saying yes, he kissed her through her ultra-thin panties. Yes, it was a distraction. A rather nice distraction, but Natalie didn't give in to it.

She caught onto Rick's chin and lifted it so they'd make eye contact. Unfortunately, she had tears in her eyes so she had a little trouble seeing him.

"I love you, too, Rick."

Relief relaxed the muscles in his face. "Hallelujah. Now, we have a reason to celebrate." And to seal the deal, he kissed her mouth.

"So, you'll marry me and have sex with me next week?" he asked.

She nodded. Maybe even earlier sex because a week suddenly seemed an eternity. "But the Harley name will require more discussion." She took a deep breath. "A lot of things will probably require discussion." With his mouth still close to hers, she made a sweeping glance around the room.

"Everything's negotiable," he said, obviously sensing where this was going. "We can live here. Or not. We can live at my house. Or not."

"You're making this easy." She smiled through the happy tears.

Rick shrugged, pulled her into his arms and held her close. "Cars, furnishings, lifestyles—all negotiable. The only thing that's not negotiable is the love."

Well, that wasn't an issue. Natalie had loved Rick a long time, and she knew their love would continue for a lifetime.

* * * * *

Turn the page for an exclusive preview of
Haunted Echoes *by Cindy Dees.*
Out next month.

Haunted Echoes

by
Cindy Dees

Robert Fraser slid the heavy backpack of books off his shoulders and set it on the stone floor with a solid thunk beside his motorcycle helmet. Letting his Scots roots show, he said, "Top o' the mornin' to ye, Lorraine. How goes it?"

The art department's blue-haired secretary and unofficial matriarch looked up from her desk. "You have a visitor. You'd better clean yourself up. Toot soo-weet."

Her bad French for "right away," liberally accented with the round vowels of Edinburgh, made him wince. "*I* have a visitor? Who is it?"

"Some old guy. Very mysterious. Came in the back door and disappeared into the chairman's office about twenty minutes ago. Professor McManus has been buzzing me to ask if you were in yet about every two minutes. Angus is in a fair tizzy over this gent, so he must be a personage with a purse, if you catch my meaning."

Angus McManus in a tizzy? The old geezer was usually

half-comatose these days. No retirement for that bloke, no sir. He'd die at his post, old Angus. The art history department he chaired at Edinburgh University was his life. Robert sighed. Sometimes he wondered if he was fated to end up the same way, shriveled and musty, hunched over tattered old books and half-assed papers from snotty graduate students.

"Go on in, luv, and rescue Angus before he has a stroke."

Robert sighed again. Schmoozing rich patrons—hell of a way to start the day. He dropped his black leather jacket on top of his rucksack, straightened his knitted tie and headed in to Angus's office. It was a spacious corner room with beautiful oak wainscoting on the walls and good light, although the books stacked absolutely everywhere ruined the sense of space entirely. Apparently, Angus didn't believe in that new-fangled invention known as the bookshelf.

"Robert, my boy!" boomed a white-haired little gnome from behind a huge walnut desk that all but swallowed him.

Angus must've lost his hearing aids again. "Good morning, Professor McManus," Robert shouted as he wended his way between piles of books.

"Was just singing your praises. Come in. Come in. Sit."

Robert crossed through a shaft of dust-filled sunlight and headed for a chair in front of the desk. He sank down onto a humped leather seat so old and slippery he had to plant his feet firmly on the floor not to slide out of it.

"Professor Fraser, this is…errm, yes, well…a patron of the arts," Angus bellowed.

Robert nodded at the silver-haired man seated quietly beside Angus's desk. The man's face was hidden in shadow, but the hawk-nosed profile and strong jaw were visible. The guy's suit looked like Armani. A wealthy art collector, then. Looking for recommendations on a purchase perhaps?

"How d'you do?" Robert said.

"Fine, thank you," the man answered cordially enough. A

slight accent of the continent lurked behind the precise English, but its nationality eluded Robert. Too faint to identify. And the man didn't offer his name. Odd. The man just sat there, studying him.

"What can we do for you today?" Robert finally asked. He hated having to work at conversations like this.

"I need the provenance of an item traced. A work of art."

Ahh. That, he could handle. He nodded and said, "Then you've come to the right place. I teach both classes here at the university on tracing the history of artwork. Usually, it's a simple matter of accessing the Getty Museum's or Interpol's databases of registered works of art. Between the two of them, they maintain provenance histories on most of the valuable pieces of art in the world."

"This piece will not be listed with either," the man said with quiet certainty.

Robert kept his facial expression neutral. A stolen work, perhaps? Coming out of hiding after a long time? A Nazi piece? Maybe even a new find? An involuntary ripple of anticipation passed through him. He dreamed of unearthing a lost masterpiece someday. Aloud, he said, "If no provenance work has been done on a piece, the research requirements can be quite extensive. And expensive, I must add."

The shadowed gentleman waved a dismissive hand, and Robert saw that it was bony and heavily veined, mottled with age spots. The man was older than his profile gave away. "Price is no object," the stranger growled.

Well, then. Blokes usually wouldn't invest unlimited funds in tracing a work unless it was worth a great deal more than they were about to spend verifying its authenticity or ownership. He leaned forward in his seat. "Tell me about the piece."

"First, you must agree to trace it for me."

"You wish to pay the costs of the provenance search, then?"

The man didn't answer. Instead, he reached inside his suit to an interior breast pocket and pulled out a checkbook.

Robert did some fast math on how much money to ask for up front when this guy pulled out a pen and poised it over a blank check.

But the man surprised him by pushing the entire black leather checkbook across the desk to him. "That is a numbered Swiss bank account. It has fifty thousand dollars U.S. in it. If it runs out of money, it will be replenished. As I said, price is no object. Will you do the job for me?"

His palms itched to take the checkbook and get out of this jail. To hit the road once more in search of adventure and fortune. To toss off the yoke of classes and papers and the boredom of academia and do what he loved best. Chase treasure. On this guy's penny, no less.

But his last brush with the law slowed him down in accepting that checkbook. A year in prison will do that to a guy. Accessory to grand theft. Reduced sentence for testifying against the ringleaders, out early for good behavior and his police record sealed. But nonetheless, enough to still his hand at his side.

"Is it stolen?" he asked bluntly.

"Not by me," the man retorted.

Robert peered into the shadows. If only he could see the guy's eyes more clearly. No way to judge if the man was lying or not. He sounded genuinely indignant at the suggestion.

The man added, "All I want you to do is find out where it came from. Who has owned it before? Who made it?"

There was nothing illegal in that. Still, his internal radar was sending him red lights and warning Klaxons over this man and his secretive request.

"Who are you?" Robert asked.

"I am a patron of the arts. I wish for my identity to be kept secret. There are those who would try to kill me if they knew I was looking into the history of this object."

Object. Not a painting, then. Damned if his mind wasn't already spinning off on the possibilities of what the object was. Pre-Roman antiquities were hot right now. Lots of pottery and jewelry coming onto the market. Maybe something from the Far East. China was dumping a lot of old stuff onto the market at ridiculously inflated prices. The thing Westerners didn't seem to grasp is thousand-year-old trinkets are a dime a dozen in that ancient land. Just because it was old didn't make it valuable.

"If you take this job, you must not reveal my existence to anyone for any reason. You could, quite literally, cost me my life." The stranger surprised him by standing up abruptly and beginning to loosen his tie.

What the hell? The guy peeled back his crisply starched shirt to reveal sparse white chest hairs and dry, wrinkled skin. But that wasn't what captured Robert's attention. Rather, it was the fist-sized scar, angry red and nastily puckered directly over the old man's heart.

"This is what happened the last time my enemies caught up with me. You must promise to keep your silence about me."

Robert blinked. That was a bullet wound or he was the Easter Bunny! "Am I going to be in danger if I take this job?"

The man finished buttoning his shirt and adjusting his tie. He sat down, his face disappearing into the shadows once more. "Would it matter if you are?"

Hullo. How did this guy know that about him? Robert *did* love the rush that came with risk. But ever since he'd come to Edinburgh University, he'd been doing his damnedest to suppress it. Either the man was phenomenally perceptive or he'd done his homework on Robert Fraser. Either way, the adrenaline junkie in Robert was aroused. Hungry. Demanding.

Down, Tonto. We're not doing anything stupid anymore.

"How will I communicate my findings to you?" Robert asked. Had he just said that? Was he actually considering taking this job? A surge of adrenaline hit him almost as hard as an orgasm. Damn, the rush felt good. Had he really let himself go that dead inside for the last couple years? Somewhere, buried deep beneath the sexual thrill, was the tiny voice of his common sense telling him to get up and walk out of here.

"All in good time. First, you must accept the job. On my terms."

Robert stared at the man. Hesitated a few more seconds. *Aww, what the hell.*

He reached out and took the checkbook. The eel skin was cool and smooth beneath his fingertips. "What am I looking for?"

FREE!

4 Books
and a surprise gift!

We would like to take this opportunity to thank you for reading this Mills & Boon® book by offering you the chance to take FOUR more specially selected titles from the Intrigue series absolutely FREE! We're also making this offer to introduce you to the benefits of the Mills & Boon® Reader Service™—

- ★ **FREE home delivery**
- ★ **FREE gifts and competitions**
- ★ **FREE monthly Newsletter**
- ★ **Exclusive Reader Service offers**
- ★ **Books available before they're in the shops**

Accepting these FREE books and gift places you under no obligation to buy, you may cancel at any time, even after receiving your free shipment. Simply complete your details below and return the entire page to the address below. You don't even need a stamp!

YES! Please send me 4 free Intrigue books and a surprise gift. I understand that unless you hear from me, I will receive 6 superb new titles every month for just £3.10 each, postage and packing free. I am under no obligation to purchase any books and may cancel my subscription at any time. The free books and gift will be mine to keep in any case.

17ZEF

Ms/Mrs/Miss/Mr ....Initials..................................

BLOCK CAPITALS PLEASE

Surname ....

Address...

....

....Postcode.....................

Send this whole page to:
UK: FREEPOST CN81, Croydon, CR9 3WZ